RUSSIA NEVER SLEEPS

RUSSIA NEVER SLEEPS

KIMBERLY O'NEILL

Copyright

Copyright © 2019 Kimberly O'Neill

ISBN: 978-1-9990943-0-0
ASIN: B07QFBSZ1T

Contact author at: koneillwriter@yandex.com
Cover photo and design by: Kimberly O'Neill
(Statue from "Children are the Victims of Adults' Vices", created by Mihail Chemiakin)

Other Books by This Author

PROPHECIES SERIES

The Prophecy of Constantinople

The Age of Erra

Tomb of the Fallen King

The Covenant of Light

AXIOM SERIES

The Axiom Cipher

Axiom Ascension

Axiom Revelation

Axiom Kingdom Come

OTHERS

Russia Never Sleeps

The Gospel of Amare

Poetic Inception

Carousel: A Collection of Dark Short Stories

WRITTEN AS DAWN O'NEILL
(EROTICA/ROMANCE FICTION)

DESCENDANTS OF POSEIDIA

Remember Me

Dream Walker

THE NEW REVOLUTION SERIES

Resistance is Futile

Resistance is Rising

Resistance is Spawned

Resistance is Evolution

Resistance is Growing

OTHERS

Room Mates

Foreign Affair

Contents

MOSCOW 1952

Part One

The Interrogator

Chapter One

The 1935 tatra 82 SUV bumped through ice and muddy slush as it pulled around the exterior of the compound situated solemnly within the clearing. Two stories of windows dotted the plain exterior of the main building. Valery adjusted his coat as he stepped out of the truck, the stiff collar and brass buttons pushed up under his chin. He pulled his cap down over his forehead and slammed the door behind him.

Efim slinked out of the passenger seat, slammed the door and skipped through the snow to catch up. "Welcome to Sukhanovka, Comrade Nikitin."

Valery glanced at the chipped plaster and boarded windows. "It's unlike anything I've seen."

"It used to be a monastery."

Three feet of snow settled the bare landscape surrounding the monastic buildings. Their feet crunched in the silence, breaking through ice. A window suppressed muffled screams above their heads as Valery kicked his boots against the doorframe, loosening snow before he entered. A prisoner knelt upright facing the wall just inside the door, holes worn through his pants. A second stood obediently next to a pitcher of water, shivering. The guard in the immediate office glanced up and acknowledged Efim as they passed. Valery removed his hat and tucked it neatly under his arm as they continued down the hall.

"There are sixty-eight interrogation cells located on these two floors." He paused and looked at Valery from the corner of his eye.

"There is also a basement. The second building is just prisoner housing."

Heels dug into the wood floor, echoing down the long hallway. Doors lined the walls, some with small windows. Ahead, a guard lit a cigarette; he turned toward the two men and with a nod acknowledged their presence. He opened the door into an old prayer room, one guard lay asleep on a couch, and another sat at a desk writing frantically. Across from them, a prisoner stood in bare feet, tattered clothing and a blood soaked face.

Valery stopped and looked in. "What is he writing?"

The guard paused. "A confession."

"That prisoner confessed?"

"No. But he will."

The door clicked shut.

Shouts, cries, slaps and thumps seeped from under doors and into the hall. Valery continued to stare ahead down the stark interior. The door at the end of the first floor read *Deputy Minister of State Security*.

"Here you will find, Comrade Ryumin. He is in charge of Sukhanovka. You will take all your orders directly from him."

Efim gave a quick tap on the door then stepped back to wait. The door flung open, unveiling a man in his forties, looking dishevelled in a collared shirt, trousers and combat boots. Breathing heavily, he slicked his long brown hair back off his forehead and looked up.

"Ah, Efim, you've returned."

"Comrade Ryumin, I would like to introduce you to Valery Nikitin."

Ryumin stripped a leather glove from his hand and held it out for Valery to shake. Over the Minister's shoulder a bloodied cloth was being removed from the floor, revealing a lush Persian carpet beneath.

"I was just finishing up."

Ryumin stepped back, opening the door wide as a guard dragged the bloodied body of a prisoner from within and down the hall. With a gesture of the arm, Ryumin welcomed Valery into the sybaritic office. He pulled a heavy wooden chair forward and set it in front of the thick gilded desk. Valery unbuttoned his coat and sat down silently, watching as Ryumin shuffled about trying to get himself organized. He poured two shots of vodka and sat down, pushing one glass towards Valery. The liquid swayed and settled in the glass on the desk as Ryumin swallowed his back.

Ryumin wiped his mouth, opened a drawer and pulled out a file. "I only received the telegram a few days ago announcing your transfer to our facility. It appears you have impressed your superiors."

Valery raised an eyebrow in mild amusement as Ryumin chuckled nervously. "It was my understanding, Comrade Ryumin, that while here my skills would be of greater service to the collective."

Ryumin cleared his throat and poured another shot. "Yes. That is why I will be putting you in charge of *Object 110*."

Plaster chipped away from the walls and stairs as Valery made his way down into the depths of the damp basement. He ducked under a lowered doorway nearly bumping a yellow bulb that glowed on the other side. Shadows masked the narrow hall and drain in the centre of the wet cement floor. Smells of mould, rotting wood and blood stung his nostrils.

"Under the directive of *Object 110* you may introduce whatever means necessary to achieve a desired result. You have full autonomy, Comrade Nikitin. You will find that we have already established what we like to call a *Heat Tank* and *Cooler*. Use them as you will."

"Thank you, Comrade Ryumin."

Valery stepped forward, inspecting the six separate interrogation rooms. Every wall had a different story; the drain in the centre of each room, the conclusion. Impervious, he continued to the end of the hall where his new office housed a small wooden chair and table.

Ryumin followed closely behind, nervously watching for signs of approval. "You'll have a couple days to settle in and then I can go over procedures with you before you start."

"That won't be necessary." Valery turned to Ryumin, "I'll start now."

The prisoner from Room 107 sat across the rickety table from Valery. Sweat poured from his brow, his body shook in terror. The fingers of his left hand sat neatly pinched between two plates of a vice, his other hand gripped at his forearm.

Valery's eyes glided over the prisoner's face. "It is not my wish to do this to you. You have brought this pain upon yourself. If you confess to your crimes, all this will go away."

"I already told you! I'm innocent!" The prisoner started to sob uncontrollably, pulling at his hand.

Valery tightened the vice one more notch and the prisoner screamed in pain. Sitting back down, he flipped open a folder and held up a piece of paper, quietly examining it. "According to this, you sent a telegram to a Doctor Etinger in response to private information regarding our great leader's health."

The prisoner whimpered quietly.

"Our great leader's health is of no concern to others. It is people like you obsessed with your own personal wealth that will be the downfall of our great nation. Do you deny this plotting against our great leader?"

The prisoner from Room 107 looked across the table at Valery and spit in his face. Calmly, Valery put the folder down, pulled a handkerchief from inside his breast pocket and wiped the spit from his face. He slid his chair back discreetly, stood and stuffed the square back inside his coat.

"It's unfortunate that you have chosen not to cooperate."

With the heel of his hand, Valery put the weight of his body onto the vice, closing the two plates together. The prisoner from Room 107 let out blood curdling screams as the tips of his fingers turned purple and then burst, splattering blood across Valery's face.

The prisoner sat whimpering and crying in his chair, the nails of his remaining hand scratching uselessly, trying to free the other. Valery stepped out into the hall, the door clicking shut behind him. Shouts and curses fell limply against the walls as he walked back to his office.

Efim sat in a reclined position at the desk and quickly rose to his feet when Valery entered. Muffled howls of pain echoed towards them, Efim nervously glanced in their direction. "You're just going to leave him there?"

Valery poured himself fresh water into a basin, washed his hands and then splashed water on his face. "For now." After drying his face he paused and looked up at the peeling paint and mould on the wall. "What time is it?"

Efim looked up at the roof as if he could see the sky. "Nearly sunrise."

"See that the prisoner makes it back to his room." In one swift motion he tossed the towel on his desk and grabbed his wool coat from the chair.

"You...you're leaving?"

"Tell Ryumin I'll return tomorrow."

The roads were quiet to Moscow as Valery pulled up to the front of the apartment house. Clouds hung low and grey absorbing the sunrise from the snow. Valery took in a deep breath of crisp air, letting it out slowly as he looked towards the dark windows of the second floor. Ice jammed the door as he tore it open and headed up the stairs two at a time.

Apartment 2C was the second door on the right; he inserted his key and turned the knob. The hinges squeaked intermittently with the motion, carefully he closed the door behind him. Swiftly, he unbuttoned his jacket, slid it off and hung it neatly on the hook beside the door.

Across the room, the bedroom door had been left ajar. He tipped his ear against it, held his breath and listened. Soft sounds of a human sleeping wisped out. With a nudge of his hand, the door swung in, revealing the sleeping figure of a beautiful young woman, her brown hair lay in waves across the pillow. He watched her a moment before approaching the bed. The hard leather of his boots knocked against the wood floor, stirring her.

Valery sat down on the edge of the bed and she opened her eyes. Upon recognition, she smiled. "I didn't think you'd make it home."

He gently caressed the side of her cheek and then ran his fingers through her hair. "I couldn't bear to have you wake alone."

She giggled, "I heard you coming."

His brows furrowed.

"You left your boots on." Katya pulled his hat from his head, letting a chunk of hair fall over his left eye. "How was your first day?"

"I get my own office."

Katya sat up and put his hat on her head. "You must be an important man now."

Valery smiled at her innocence, cradled her chin in his hand and drew her face forward, kissing her delicately on the lips. "Have you made plans for today?"

"I have some errands to run this morning."

"Wake me when you return."

Chapter Two

The scent of freshly baked biscuits and stew wafted through the air, stirring Valery from deep sleep. Afternoon sun glowed through the thin curtain which wavered slightly from the cold outside. Muffled tinkering in the kitchen caused him to smile. Katya was young; her child-like attempts to please him, enduring.

Valery stood leaning against the doorframe watching her. She had an apron tied around her waist, exposing her naked buttocks to him, socks on her feet. As she turned around their eyes met, causing her to nearly drop the bowl in her hands. Embarrassed, she curtsied and set the bowl down.

"I didn't hear you get up."

"I didn't expect such a celebration."

Katya untied the apron and let it fall to the floor. She sauntered over to him, ran her hands across his broad chest and began to peel off his open shirt. Valery wrapped her in his arms, grabbed her buttocks and kissed her passionately in return.

Pulling himself away from her, he closed his eyes and breathed deeply through his nose the aromas saturating the kitchen. "I'm so hungry I can't decide what to eat first."

Smacking him playfully, Katya strutted back to the table and pulled out his chair. "There will be time for dessert later."

Lying in bed, Valery twirled Katya's hair between his fingers. She nuzzled in closer, each warm breath blowing through the downy hair on his chest.

"I won't be able to see you for a couple days."

Valery stopped his fingers, her hair falling across her face.

"I think my family is beginning to suspect something."

He put his lips to her head. "Marry me."

Katya propped herself up on an elbow, staring down at his face. "What?"

"Marry me."

"But..."

"But what?"

"Well, it's not that simple," she sat up and turned to crawl out of bed.

Grabbing her arm, Valery turned her back to face him. "Why is it not that simple? We'll marry and then you can move in for good."

A single tear fell from the corner of Katya's eye; slowly it slid down her cheek and fell onto her breast.

The callas on Valery's thumb rubbed against her cheek as he wiped it away. "Think about it."

With a sniffle, she nodded.

A damp chill swept through Valery's spine as he sat at his desk flipping through the pages of a folder. The sounds of shuffling feet caused him to look up as Efim brought another prisoner down into the basement; he paused briefly before unlocking Room Four and shoving the prisoner inside. With a confident swagger he walked into the office and threw himself in the chair opposite the desk. Ignoring him, Valery continued to peruse the file.

"You need anything else?"

"No. That will be all."

Efim shifted nervously. "So, you come from Lubyanka?"

"Yes."

"Pretty nice place. Big." Efim picked a rock out of the heel of his boot. "Hard to believe you got promoted to come here." Efim looked up to find Valery watching him; he put his foot down and got up from the chair. "Well, better get going. I'll be back in a couple hours to collect the prisoner."

Valery watched Efim's shadowy figure disappear back up the stairs at the end of the hall and he tucked the folder neatly into the drawer of his desk. Stripping his military tunic off, he draped it neatly over the back of the chair. Adeptly, he unbuttoned his cuffs and rolled each sleeve up past the elbow. Grabbing his towel from the basin, he headed for Room Four.

The prisoner from Room 58 sat huddled in the corner of the room. A distinct smell of urine wafted through the air. Steam hung in a nebulous formation around the bulb in the centre of the ceiling. Valery stood before the prisoner, casting a monstrous shadow across the wall. Pulling the towel from his shoulder, he began to twist it in his hands.

"Yakov Etinger, you are being charged with forming a terrorist organization responsible for plotting against the leader of the Soviet Government under Article 58-2 and 58-8 of the Russian Soviet Federative Socialist Republic Penal Code. I have been instructed to collect evidence on behalf of Minister Abakumov. Do you deny sending a telegram to a Doctor Vovsi in regards to personal details of our great leader's health?"

Squinting from the glow of yellow light in a halo around Valery, Etinger stared at him. "I recognize you." He crawled to his knees exposing his thin frame and shielded his eyes with his hand.

Dark bushy hair and a thick moustache covered the rest of his face. "Yes, in Moscow. You used to work at Lubyanka...in the basement."

Valery held out the towel. "I could force this towel down your throat and into your stomach. Once there, it would absorb the acid and attach itself to the lining. It's a painful way to die, having your stomach ripped from your mouth."

Etinger stared from the towel, to Valery's eyes. "Yes, I believe you are right." He sat back down, cross-legged on the floor, leaning against the wall. "Perhaps you will spare an old man such humility and sit with him for a while. I will tell you whatever you want to know."

The towel dropped from Valery's right hand and untwisted.

"Have you ever heard of Martemyan Ryutin?"

Standing frozen under the heat of the bulb, Valery eyed Etinger.

"Have you ever questioned an order before? Sometimes, people are wrong." He shrugged his shoulders, staring at the floor.

A puff of mist escaped Valery's mouth with each breath as he stood strong, watching.

Curling into a ball, Etinger shivered uncontrollably, holding his bare feet in his hands to warm them. "Our Country is sick. Any who oppose her master are caged like animals and left to die. We need a cure. Ryutin had a cure once and they shut him up, just like they shut anyone up. It doesn't matter anymore, we're all going to die. Even you."

The door slammed shut, leaving the prisoner behind.

Large flakes of snow fell quietly to the ground. Valery stomped across the compound towards a group of trees on the other side. He buttoned his coat and put on a pair of leather gloves from his pocket. A bush rustled, knocking snow from the branches to the ground as another guard stepped out from behind it, buttoning up his trousers.

Startled, the guard jumped to attention, his pants falling around his ankles. "Sir!"

"Why aren't you at your post?"

His knees shook in the cold as Valery looked him over and continued through the trees. Embarrassed, he pulled his trousers up and followed. A few feet away, they stopped at a group of wooden boxes set neatly in the snow.

"They're pretty quiet today." The guard kicked a box with the toe of his boot.

"Open number five."

The guard pulled a key from his pocket and unlocked the lid of the box. The hinges squeaked as he flung the lid back. Inside, a man lay curled in a fetal position, his face squinted as light flooded the interior.

Valery peered inside. "Is your name Vovsi?"

The prisoner nodded.

"Bring him to Room Six." Without waiting for a response, he turned and headed back.

The door to Room Six clicked shut behind Valery and he headed back to his office. He stopped in the doorway when he saw Ryumin sitting in his chair reading through the report on his desk.

"You think these two prisoners were working together?"

"They have admitted it."

Ryumin put the papers down. "Good work, Comrade Nikitin." He tossed Valery a towel.

Valery caught it and began to wipe the blood from his arms. "They still have not confessed to their crimes. Their faith cannot be broken."

"You've been here for days. Go home and rest."

"I'll file my report with Abakumov when I return to Moscow."

Ryumin approached Valery and grasped his shoulder as he passed by. "No doubt they'll get off easy and be sent to the Gulag."

To think that the Gulag would be considered a haven when compared to the hands of Valery Nikitin.

Exhausted, Valery stalked up the stairs hanging his head, his feet heavy. The Minister's door stood open as he walked passed, Ryumin sat at his desk throwing back a shot of vodka. He spotted Valery and leaned forward in his chair. "Come! Have a drink with me!"

Raising his hand, Valery waved him off and continued down the hall. Katya crept into his thoughts as the sounds of a woman screaming obscenities sprang from under a door. His feet stopped. He held his breath and listened, but the voices were too muffled. He wiped his face with his hand and chuckled to himself before continuing down the hall.

Chapter Three

The apartment lay empty and quiet as he turned on the light in the kitchen. Too tired to think of food, he turned it off and headed to the bedroom. Valery sat on the edge of the bed and stared out the window at the lit apartment across the street. A family bustled about preparing for dinner. A child was setting the table. He kicked off his shoes and lay down.

On the edge of sleep, a pounding thundered from his apartment door. His eyes sprang open, his body numb and disoriented. The door pounded again. Shaking from exhaustion, Valery dumped himself onto his feet and stumbled to the door, turning on the kitchen light along the way.

The door thundered again and he swung it open. A young man in his mid-twenties stood on the other side. The ushanka on his head sad dishevelled, one flap hanging down. The holes in his valenki books had been filled in with mud and snow. He was breathing heavy, clutching at his hands. Valery stared at him, watching the boy's eyes spring wide in reverence.

"I...I'm a friend of Katya's."

Valery's figure filled the doorframe.

"My name is Taras. She told me that you work for Deputy Ryumin."

He stood tall, towering over the fidgeting boy. His silent gaze locked onto him.

"They took her."

Valery blinked his eyes as if waking from a dream.

The boy stuttered. "Th…they took her. The NKVD, they stormed our meeting and just started arresting people. Th…they took Katya."

"What meeting?" Valery said, finding his voice.

"I've been waiting for two days for you to return. She said you would be able to help."

"Help do what?"

"Get her out. I'm not sure where they took her. First it was Lubyanka, but my scout told me they moved her yesterday."

Grabbing the kid by the collar, Valery pulled him forward, their faces nearly touching. "I could crush your throat with my bare hand!" He threw the kid to the floor and slammed the door shut.

Valery paced the apartment, fear, anger and confusion swirled through his thoughts. The woman's voice from the prison echoed in his memory. He stuffed his feet into his boots, swung his coat over his shoulders and pulled his hat down on his forehead as he stormed out of the apartment.

The door to his truck groaned as he tore it open, he threw himself onto the seat and slammed it shut. He sat idle, breathing heavily as mist swirled from his mouth in tiny clouds. Fumbling in his pocket, he grabbed the keys and started the truck.

The hum of the engine was soothing during the long drive back to Sukhanovka. Icy roads caused the truck to skid, Valery let up on the pedal. The leather from his gloves squeaked against the wheel as his hands squeezed it tightly.

Pulling into the compound, Valery drove the truck up to the main building. Like beacons, the headlights lit the path to the entrance. He slammed the door behind him, rocking the truck from the force. He glanced up at the stars sparkling against the clear black sky before turning back, letting out a deep relaxing breath, and grasping the door knob.

Stepping over a prisoner lying face down in the hall, Valery turned and entered the main office. The administrative officer lay hunched over his desk, asleep. Valery's foot shot out and kicked the desk, waking the officer with a start.

"I need the admittance registry from two days ago."

"Yes, Comrade Nikitin." The officer sprung to his feet and began searching through a cabinet. Successfully, he yanked the file from the drawer and handed it over triumphantly.

Valery snatched the folder from his hands and looked over the registry of names. Katya's name jumped from the page, he blinked in shock. Taking note of her room assignment, he closed the folder, handed it back, then turned and walked out of the room.

Efim stumbled from an interrogation room with another guard, both drunk. Recognizing Valery, they quickly tried to jump to attention. Ignoring their intoxication, Valery marched passed shouting over his shoulder, "Bring me the prisoner from Room 78!"

With his back to the hall, Valery stood silently, waiting. Footsteps thundered down the stairs as Efim dragged the prisoner into the basement. Small female whimpers escaped the prisoner's lips, a potato sack over her head.

"Put her in the Heat Tank!" his voiced echoed down the hall.

Efim threw open the door and shoved her inside, slamming it shut. Katya sprang to her feet, her fists pounding on the door, her shouts futile.

Pulling out his chair, Valery sat himself down and flipped open her file. Efim stumbled forward, collapsing into the chair opposite him. "I heard the boys upstairs say that she's part of some underground branch of the International Communist League."

Valery let out a sigh and continued reading.

"She's feisty. It took a bit of work, but Yan was able to beat some sense into her."

Without looking up, Valery remarked, "I'll call you when I'm done."

Too drunk to care, Efim pried himself from the chair and stumbled away.

Chapter Four

Four hours later, Valery put the folder down and glanced down the hall. The basement had grown silent. Like a ritual, he removed his wool coat and hung it over the back of the chair. Neatly he unbuttoned his tunic, removed it and hung it over the jacket. One by one, he unbuttoned his cuffs and rolled up his sleeves.

The green paint on the door was chipped and peeling, revealing the grey wood beneath. With his key, he undid the padlock and swung the latch aside. The brass knob was black and sticky beneath his palm as he turned it and stepped into the room.

A wave of heat washed over his body, trying to escape through the open door. As he shut it, the room fell still. Mould dotted the roof, gathered in clumps where moisture dripped to the floor. The glow of the bulb cast a sickly yellow guise across the walls.

Katya lay face down in the centre of the cement floor trying to keep cool. Her dress was soaked through with sweat. Strands of hair stuck to her face as she raised her head from the floor. Valery remained by the door undisturbed. As she looked up, recognition crossed her face and her eyes took on a renewed hope.

"Val? Is that you? You came for me."

Valery bit his lip, remaining still.

Katya crawled to a seated position and stared up at him. "What is it? What has happened?"

"Who is Taras?"

"He...he's a friend. Just a friend. Can I have some water, please? It's so hot in here. Why do they keep it so hot?" With no response, she crawled to her knees to get a better look at his face. "Why are you asking me this?"

His face softened. "This is what I do."

"What? No. You said you worked for Deputy Ryumin. You said you watched over prisoners. But here...here..." A look of horror crossed her face.

As she scrambled away from him Valery noticed dark purple and black welts all over her legs. His face cringed with the knowledge of how they got there. He took a step forward and hesitated a moment. "Katya..."

"No! Stay away from me! You're a monster!" Huddling against the wall she began to cry. She turned back to him and shakily crawled to her feet. "How many people have you killed?"

Valery stood back as if she had slapped him across the face. Before he knew it, he stood before her and swung the back of his hand against hers. "Whore! You are a disgrace to the people of this country who have sacrificed themselves in the name of the republic!"

Falling to the floor, Katya clutched at her face, cowering. Waiting for the next blow.

The wall shook, rattling the doors along its face as Valery stormed down the hall back to his office.

Startled by the commotion, Efim ran down the stairs. "What happened? Is everything alright?"

Valery turned to Efim his brow furrowed, the creases on his forehead white from tension.

"They said she was feisty, but I wouldn't have thought she could break you."

The irises of his eyes swelled to two large black points. "Leave me," he growled between gritted teeth.

"Sure you don't want me to –"

"Now."

As if leaving a throne room, Efim grabbed the edge of his hat and bowed forward, stepped back, then turned and continued down the hall.

Valery marched across Dzerzhinsky Square, ice crunched under his feet. The five floors of the Commissariat for Internal Affairs rose up towards the sky. A clock sat neatly centred at the roof reading 2:24pm. Pale green walls cast a hue over the Palladian floors. Footsteps echoed along long corridors and shuffled upstairs.

Sitting stoically in the hall, Valery waited as the low grumblings of Abakumov sifted through the wall, broken up by female giggles. Rustling and grunting leaked under the door and quickly faded. A young girl, her blonde hair loosely pinned atop her head, squeezed out the door. She shifted her dress and smoothed her skirt. Turning, she caught Valery's broad figure in her eye. Blushing, she scurried by, the click of her heels echoing like the pop of gunfire.

The hall became silent. Ten minutes passed before he was able to pry himself from the chair and stand before Abakumov's door. He raised his hand tentatively as he inhaled deeply, his knock echoed strongly.

"Yes?" The raspy voice of Abakumov sounded tired.

Hand grasped knob and turned. The door swung out and Valery stepped inside.

Abakumov looked up from his desk, the glow of light from the window reflecting off his exposed forehead. A large nose protruded from his clean-shaven face. Thick dark eyebrows hovered over large eyes. A once tall thin figure now sat hunched and saggy over a desk.

"Ah, Nikitin."

Valery sat opposite the desk and pulled the folder from under his arm, placing it neatly before Abakumov. "I have gathered what evidence I was able to extract from Etinger. He was surprisingly more cooperative than I expected."

Abakumov grunted and moved the folder aside. "Good."

Eyes darted from the folder to Abakumov. "Would you like me to press them further?"

"That won't be necessary, you've done your job. Set up transport for them back to Lubyanka."

"Yes, sir." An awkward silence filled the room, Valery rose and headed for the door.

"Good work, Nikitin," Abakumov remarked offhandedly.

Valery paused briefly before closing the door quietly behind him.

Two guards stood outside the main door at Sukhanovka leaning against the wall. Cigarette smoke swirled through the snowflakes gliding to the ground. A heavy silence hung from the grey clouds overhead. Soft snow caked to Valery's boots as they squeaked in the cold. The guards shuffled aside, letting him pass.

Neglecting the melting snow, he continued towards the stairs at the end of the hall. Puddles in the shape of boot prints trailed behind him. Hearty laughter sprang from an open interrogation room; Efim glanced up meeting Valery's eyes as he passed. The laughter broke off and he quickly ran after him down the hall.

"Comrade Nikitin!"

Valery ignored him, hulking on.

"Comrade Nikitin! I thought you might want to know, that girl, she's dead!"

The soles of his boots stuck to the floor.

"She died last night. Yan and the boys worked her over pretty good. Stubborn bitch just wouldn't talk."

His heavy foot pried loose from the floor, taking a step forward, then stopped.

"She had a message for you before she died. She said, 'Tell Val I'm sorry and that I will always love him.' Why do you think she said that?" Efim smirked.

Eyes hard as stone turned and set their gaze on Efim. The guard shifted uneasily from the stare. Valery began back in his direction, heels digging into the floor in a march of vengeance. He stopped, his lips skimming Efim's face. "Is there something you'd like to say to me?"

"N...no, sir. I...I just thought you'd want to know."

Hands clenched into fists at his side, fingernails piercing the skin. His jaw clenched, the pressure causing the vein on his forehead to throb. "I suggest you keep this to yourself, Efim. The consequences could be detrimental to your health." Valery stepped back and began to turn away.

"Who was she to you?" The question hung in the air waiting for an answer.

Valery inclined his head. "Someone who made me feel human once."

The stairs at the end of the hall could not come fast enough as Valery staggered into the basement. His hand shot out, shattering the yellow bulb above his head. Cast into a dark pit, he treaded forward, gently swinging the office door shut behind him. A wave of anger swelled. The chair behind his desk shattered against the wall where he threw it. The basin of water splashed to the floor, followed by the crashing of his desk.

Valery tore through the snow across the compound. He gasped, stumbled, crawled back to his feet and disappeared into the trees. Time ceased as he began to run, branches shot out, tearing at his face. Out of breath, he collapsed into the snow on his knees. Bare hands plunged forward, vanishing beneath an icy crust.

Tears caught in his throat as his body convulsed in sobs. Mucus dripped from his nose. His hat fell off as his forehead dipped forward. Melting snow soaked through his pants. A soft white clump slipped from a branch landing with a muffled thump in the distance. Tears began to stream down his cheeks, dripping and merging with the icy ground. Nausea grumbled in his stomach before rising up his throat, burning as it projected in a steaming splatter against the white snow.

Images of Katya's smiling face flashed through his memories. The silky smooth skin of her arms and legs. The soft flowing waves of her hair cascading across slim shoulders. Why did she do it? Why did she betray him? Why did she die? And why did his heart hurt so bad? The pain in his chest with each breath burned down his spine.

Chapter Five

Shivering, Valery jostled the door closed behind him. The wet soles of his boots slipped, causing him to nearly trip over the prisoner lying face down on the floor.

The administrative officer thrust his head out into the hall. "Comrade Nikitin, the Minister would like to speak with you."

Valery inclined his head. Red swollen eyes glared down the hall.

Ryumin's door bore down on him as he stood before it. He tapped on it with his knuckle before pushing it open. The Minister sat at his desk, a cigarette in one hand, a shot of vodka in the other as he read an open file.

"Ah, Nikitin. You look like you've been working too hard. Sit. You'll have to be more careful in the future." He swallowed the shot back and set the glass aside.

Lifting an eyebrow, Valery shot Ryumin a look.

"I'll see to it that the items in your office get replaced this time, but I suggest that in the future, you make sure you conduct all your business within an interrogation cell."

A sigh of relief escaped his lips and he hunched forward, resting against the arm of the chair.

"Abakumov sent over another prisoner for you. He wants you to start immediately. Grinshtein, a neuropathologist. Seems they were planning something big. It should be easy for you, he's already been in the Gulag for a while."

Grinshtein sat hunched over in the chair unconscious, his wrists and ankles bound with rope. Blood dripped from his fingertips. Valery stepped back letting the pliers fall from his hand. In the dim light black liquid spackled the walls and trickled down to the floor. A small pool of the sticky substance inched towards his foot, he moved away letting it slide into the drain.

Uncontrollably he began to heave. Bracing his hands on his knees he vomited onto the floor. With the back of his hand he wiped his mouth and looked up at the prisoner. The man's face lay relaxed, pressed up against his shoulder. His chest rose slowly up, then down. Feeling faint, Valery left the room, leaning against the door in the hall.

Dragging his feet, he tore his wool coat from his desk. Swinging it across his shoulders he headed up the stairs, nearly knocking Efim over on the way.

"What's the matter with you?"

Ignoring the taunt, he lunged up the remaining stairs. The long coat flew open behind him like a cape as he wisped down the hall. His feet kicked the door as it opened and then slammed shut behind him.

The compound sat empty and quiet. Valery edged his way to the rear of the building before stopping and throwing his back against the wall. He pulled a cigarette from his pocket and slid down to the ground. A heavy object from inside his coat thumped against his chest as he leaned back against the wall.

Ryumin took a puff from his cigarette shaking ashes onto the papers in his hands. Shostakovich's Symphony No.2 played quietly over the radio. A gunshot rang out from beyond the window. He looked up and paused, taking notice of the compound outside. Placing

39

the cigarette back in his mouth, he leaned across his desk and turned the volume up.

Efim's eyes sprang open and he sat up from the couch with a start as the sounds of gunfire echoed through the building. Stumbling to his feet, he flew out the door, knocking his shoulder against the frame. His heavy boots thundered down the hall towards the exit. The administrative officer skidded to a halt in the foyer and the two men nearly collided. Efim shoved him aside and sprang out the door. After a few feet he stopped abruptly and tried to get his bearings, the other officer crashing into him from behind.

Shouts rang out from across the compound as a guard pointed towards the rear of the main building. Efim dashed off, tripping through the three feet of snow blanketing the ground. As he rounded the corner, Valery's broad back stood in sharp contrast against the white background. His back sat hunched and his head hung heavy. Efim strained to try and get a good look, noticing the snow at Valery's feet had turned a red.

"Comrade Nikitin!"

Valery remained still, not willing to turn around.

"Comrade Nikitin, is everything alright?"

Valery breathed a deep sigh and stood, before turning around to face the two men. Grasped tightly in his right hand, a gun; blood dripped from the swaying carcass of a dead rabbit in the other.

Ice cracked under the wheels of the truck as Valery pulled up to the apartment house. He sat with the engine idling, hands gripping the wheel. A knock on the passenger side window broke the atmosphere and his head snapped to the side. Taras smiled awkwardly and waved. Valery turned the engine off, grunted, and exited the vehicle.

"Comrade Nikitin!"

Valery stood by the hood of the truck, staring at the boy.

Taras balked, waiting for Valery to approach. When he didn't, he took a step forward. "Have you heard any news?"

Brushing past the boy, Valery headed for the apartment house. "She's dead."

"What?" He reached out and grabbed Valery's shoulder.

Swinging around, he knocked the boy down onto the sidewalk. "I said, she's dead."

"What did you do?" He scrambled to his feet.

"What did *I* do?" Hand clutched throat and pulled Taras forward. "If it wasn't for you, she wouldn't have been at that meeting." He threw the boy back.

"Me? Did it ever occur to you that maybe she wanted to be there?"

Leather creaked as Valery clenched his fists. His eyes darted about the quiet street. An old lady hobbled down the sidewalk wrapped in fur. Taras stood still, afraid to move. A black car slowly made its way down the street, the two occupants inside watching suspiciously as it passed.

Taras grabbed Valery by the elbow. "Maybe we should go somewhere and talk?"

Ripping his arm away, Valery looked up at the second floor windows, the truck, and then up and down the empty street. His eyes rested on Taras, holding his gaze. "Did you love her?"

"What?" The young man's face morphed into shock.

"Katya. Did you love her?"

The boy dug his hands into his pockets. "I...we...it wasn't like that. Look, if you're wondering if she loved you, well, she did. You were all she ever talked about. She wished she could tell you about our meetings, but she knew you would never approve."

"She lied to me."

"No. Katya would never lie. She was protecting you."

"Protecting me? From what?"

Taras turned around as the black car made a second pass. "Come on." He grabbed Valery and edged him down the street. They ducked down an alley and continued until they reached the Moskva River. Heading down Moskvoretskaya Street, the onion-shaped peaks of Pokrovskiy Cathedral towered above the rooftops. Plodding through Krasnaya Square under a grey sky, they stopped under the bronze arm of Minin's Monument.

"Katya told me about your transfer to Sukhanovka. I have heard rumours about that prison." Leaning against the monument he pulled his collar up around his neck.

"Have you." Valery's face remained stoic.

A gentle snowfall wisped across the empty square. The city was silent; its citizens huddled in their beds.

"Only members of the ICL know where and when our meetings are being held. After the NKVD stormed our last one, I did some asking around."

Shoving his hands in his pockets, Valery shuffled his feet in the snow, listening.

"The NKVD has spies everywhere. Did anyone know about you and Katya?"

"No." Valery paused. "Yes. A man I work with at the prison. He said Katya told him about me during an interrogation."

"Did anyone know about your relationship before?"

"No." He turned to Taras. "You did."

"I know what you're thinking, but I would never betray Katya like that."

"She trusted you."

"Yes."

"Why didn't you tell her what I did at the prison?"

Taras met Valery's eyes. "She loved you. I could never take that from her."

Valery turned away, staring out across the square. His eyes fell to his boots. "She made me feel like what I was doing meant something, like I was a part of something. I felt like it was my duty to my country." He turned back to Taras. "Now, I'm not so sure. She took that from me. I failed her."

An engine growled in the night, growing louder as the black car sped across the square. Snow and ice spun out from under the wheels causing the vehicle to skid.

Over Valery's shoulder, Taras spied the vehicle coming towards them. "Shit."

Valery spun around as the car came to a stop. Two men dressed in long, black, double-breasted wool coats exited and began to approach on foot. With guns raised, they stopped a few feet from the monument. A third man scampered out of the car and strutted in their direction.

Stepping forward, Valery made a point of flashing his Ministry of Internal Affairs emblem on his arm.

One of the men stepped forward, pointing his weapon at Valery. "Valery Nikitin?"

"Yes."

"You have been found guilty of being a member of the Vory v Zakone and of conspiring with known members of the Left Opposition of the International Communist League."

"What?"

"Turn around and get on your knees."

Valery turned around and faced Taras. "What is this about?"

"I don't know." Taras stood frozen against the monument.

A shot rang out and Taras fell to the ground. A pool of blood oozed onto the snow underneath his body.

"Place your hands behind your back."

Valery did as he was told, watching the dark liquid spread through the snow and trickle across a patch of ice. The officer grabbed his arms holding his hands tight behind his back.

Approaching footsteps crunched in the silence and stopped behind Valery. "Comrade Nikitin."

The officer pulled Valery to his feet and spun him around. "You."

Part Two

Lone Wolf

Chapter Six

Efim stood with a smirk on his face. "I have someone who is interested in speaking with you." He motioned towards the car. "Please."

Valery glanced back at the lifeless body of Taras, the dark snow freezing in an icy crust around it. Efim stood next to the open door of the car. Shoving his hands deep in his pockets he stepped towards Efim; in the silence, all he could hear was the scrape of soles against the stone and snow under his feet.

The muffled engine hummed as the vehicle pulled away from the scene. With one last glance out the window, two men could be seen hoisting Taras's body into the back of a truck.

"You'll have to excuse the theatrics, Comrade Nikitin," Efim said, diverting Valery's attention back to him. "It seems you have made quite the legend of yourself and we wanted to be sure that you could be trusted."

"Trusted," Valery repeated, still trying to understand the day's events.

The vehicle glided through the dark streets. Valery sat in silence his eyes scanning the buildings as they swept passed his view. He caught his reflection in the window, stone grey eyes staring back at him. His face remained stoic, defined, masking the turmoil that broiled deep within.

The car came to a stop, Efim popped up the collar on his jacket before stepping out. Valery followed, his body numb to the environment around him, as he was led into a large hotel. The grand foyer within was unrecognizable, no expense spared to the lavish decor.

Polished brass, gilded wood and Persian carpets swept him deeper inside as he was led up a grand staircase.

They stopped outside two large mahogany doors. "He's waiting for you inside," Efim remarked, snapping Valery back to his present circumstance.

Steadying himself, he grasped the shiny doorknob, gave it a twist, and stepped inside.

A man in a simple suit stood by the large window across the room; he gazed out into the early morning, the sun not yet touching the horizon. His thick silvery hair was cut short and slicked back, giving him a regal appearance. He held a small glass in his hands, and Valery could just make out the faded markings of prison tattoos, telling of this man's criminal legacy.

"Please, have a seat," he said, motioning towards a chair. He glided across the room to meet Valery, seating himself opposite him. "Tell me a story." He picked up a bottle of vodka and began pouring two shots, handing one to Valery. Piercing blue eyes looked across at him, waiting.

Valery held his own shot glass, staring back.

"Please," he coaxed, "humour me. Tell me, Valery Nikitin, where did you grow up?"

"Lipetsk."

"It must have been hard living with those Germans from the air base around."

Valery shifted in his seat, the cool glass still in his hand.

"People don't forget something like war."

"No."

Silence hung in the room as both men sat staring at one another. The man swallowed back his shot and poured another. "Let me tell *you* a story, Comrade Valery, of a boy who was captured by the enemy. Tortured and punished for information. Only, this boy had no information to give." He paused, watching for any sign of reaction from Valery before continuing. "Beaten, bruised and abused, this boy watched, and he learned from his captors. He learned how to mask his emotions. He no longer could feel. And when the time came they showed him," he paused, locking eyes with Valery, "Tell me, what did they show you?"

Valery set his glass down, the clear liquid sloshing around. "What is it you want with me?"

The man gulped back his shot, the glass knocked at the table as he set it down. He looked up at Valery searching for some sign of a human being within before replying. "I want you to survive, Comrade Nikitin."

Valery blinked, taken aback. His mind drew a blank, his eyes roaming the room looking for a reply. "Survive?"

The gentleman sat back in his chair, fingers gently tapping at the table before looking up at Valery. "If I may talk plainly." He hesitated, his breath caught in his throat. "There are many of us watching with great interest the decrees of our great leader." His fingers tapped the table again as he shifted slightly in his chair, eyes pinned on Valery. "You follow your orders without question, am I correct Comrade Nikitin?"

"Without question."

"You had a girlfriend, did you not?"

His eyes dropped to the tabletop as he answered. "I did."

"I heard she recently died."

48

"Yes." The word lodged itself in his throat.

"Do you realize that if found connected to her, you too could be charged? Be purged?"

Valery inhaled deeply, his eyes locked with his questioner, searching for a sign that there was more to his inquiries.

The man chuckled. "You thought your position would protect you?" He paused and leaned forward slightly. "As I'm sure you've seen, even those in political office are without protection from our great leader."

"I do as I am ordered."

"Of course you do."

There was a long silent pause, both men observing the other.

"Paranoia and suspicion are a disease spreading through Russia. Who can we trust? Who do you trust, Comrade Valery?"

"I...." Valery's mind went blank. Trust. When did he ever have to trust? He did what he was told. The order came and he executed it. Period. But now, yes, now things had changed. There was a trust, one that had been broken the day Katya died. Whose trust?

Katya had been young when they met, only eighteen to his thirty-three.

As Valery left the Kremlin and walked across the square towards the river something bright caught his eye. The sun broke through the clouds, shrouding her in its halo like an angel. Laughter echoed towards him as he stopped and stared. As this innocent angel began to tear up her small lump of bread, breaking off pieces and throwing them towards the birds that had gathered.

The heels of Valery's boots thumped against the stone towards her. "Devushka! You there! What are you doing?"

Her laughter faded as her eyes slowly rose to meet his. Her body straightened. "I am feeding the birds."

"But that is illegal."

"Is it? Why?"

It wasn't illegal, but Valery could not think why someone would want to feed the birds. Why would they give their last piece of bread to a bird? What would she eat? She would starve. "But what will you eat if you feed it to them? People are starving, they eat birds."

"Well then I will fatten them up." Her eyes sparkled.

"Are you not afraid of starving?" Her dress hung off her lithe frame.

She shrugged her shoulders. "The birds are not afraid of starving, why should I be?"

Her manner was unusual, so carefree and so innocent to the horrors happening around her. Somehow this untainted angel had survived. She needed protection and Valery would take it upon himself to make sure that she was safe and well fed. He pulled out another chunk of bread from his pocket which he had been saving for lunch and held it out to her. "Here."

Her face lit up and then faded as her eyes tried to read his.

"For you," he clarified. "Not the birds."

A small giggle was exhaled as she took the bread from his hand. "Thank you."

He gave a curt nod and turned on his heels and began walking away. A shiver ran down his spine as he got the feeling that she was still watching him. He stopped in his tracks, heels scraping to a halt; a compelling desire to turn around and go back to her took hold of him — a sensation Valery was not accustomed to. Should he? What if she *thought him strange? What would she think of him if she knew what he did? If she knew how many people he had tortured and killed?*

With a deep inhale he calmed himself, turned and marched back to her. "I was thinking, it's not safe out here, perhaps I should walk you home."

Katya looked up from where she stood, still holding the bread in her hands. Her face froze momentarily.

"My name is Valery Nikitin. I am a Lieutenant in the Ministry of State Security." He stood tall reciting his title.

"My name is Yekaterina Dimitrievna Garina and I am a student at the Lomonosov University."

"What are you studying?"

"Economics."

"Economics? Why would you take that?"

Katya held up the bread Valery had given her. "So that everyone can afford a loaf of bread one day." She smiled. "Thank you, I must go to class now."

"Then I will walk you to your class." He watched her face become still. "That is...if you would like me to?" His voice was naturally accustomed to giving orders.

She shoved the bread into her bag as she thought. There was something about this man, something different in his mannerisms that Katya couldn't help but to be curious about. "Okay."

"Comrade Valery, who do you trust?"

Valery's eyes blinked, transporting him back to the present, staring at this strange man sitting across from him pouring another shot of vodka. "I'm not sure I understand your question."

"It is quite simple. A man of your position has committed some terrible acts. Torture, am I correct?"

"I have committed nothing. I do my job." Valery watched him chuckle as he swallowed back his shot.

"Yes, your job. And your orders, do you *trust* that they are accurate?"

"Everything is according to the law."

"It is. And you trust that the law is just?"

"It is the law. Our government and its great leader have seen to its justification."

"And you trust that their justification is for the benefit of everyone?"

"It is."

"And what if that same law found you guilty of a crime you did not commit, but you were still tortured to confess this crime? That the perpetrator of this crime was your best friend, or maybe your girlfriend, and they confessed you as the guilty perpetrator? Would that same law be just?"

"That is why we have the courts."

"But what if all evidence pointed to you, and the judge declares you guilty even though you know that you did not commit this crime?"

Valery began to open his mouth and then closed it, unable to reply.

Suddenly the door burst open and two large men entered. The first threw a twisted bedsheet around Valery's torso, securing him to the chair. The second quickly tied his hands. Valery struggled against his captors.

The unknown man silently observed, pouring himself another shot and calmly took a sip, waiting. "What would you do, Mr. Nikitin? If I ripped your finger nails out of your hand right now, what would you do? What *could* you do?" He paused, waiting for a reply. "Would you confess to a crime you did not commit?"

"I have not committed any crime."

"Tell me, Comrade Nikitin, do you follow the faith?"

Valery remained silent.

"Has the devil got your tongue?" He knocked back the rest of his shot and slammed the glass on the table. "Do you want to know what they showed me?" The man unbuttoned his shirt and held it open, revealing a web of scars which had been tattooed over with a church, crosses and a large knife stabbing his heart, two large stars beneath each shoulder. "My story is not too unlike yours, Mr. Nikitin. You see, I too survived the system of torture and abuse inflicted on me."

Valery stared at the tattoos reading the man's story. Seven cupolas on the church; he had been incarcerated seven different times. A knife in the heart – he'd lost his desire to live. An array of crosses – perhaps depicting his family. Two stars – his allegiance to a new family, the Vory v Zakone. Born from deep within the Gulag, the Vory brotherhood of thieves began in defiance to the Communist paranoia that swept the country. Working in secret, hidden deep within the prison camps and city underworld, its network grew countering government corruption with its own set of rules and laws.

"We thought we lost you, brother. Turns out, you just switched sides."

One of the men tore open Valery's clothing to reveal the tattoo reading VOHRA on his shoulder, indicating his allegiance to the NKVD.

Valery pursed his lips, tension hanging on his brow. "I hardly call it switching sides. More like self-preservation. You hardly look like a man who can judge."

"Do I?" The man leaned forward. "You have forgotten me, brother."

A lump formed in Valery's throat, his mind searching to remember. Remember something of the past he fought so long to forget. His eyes grew firm.

"Ah, there is still a memory in there, isn't there?"

"Misha...."

Misha gave the two men a nod and they released Valery, taking only one step back. "Drink with me, brother." He poured another shot of vodka and held up Valery's glass to him. "Take it."

Chapter Seven

"Go on, take it." The thin gangly man was old enough to have been his father, holding out a piece of bread for Valery. Slowly his small frozen fingers pinched the slice and lifted it to his lips for his mouth to soften. "You must be new here."

Valery nodded as he chewed. An icy wind blew the flaps on his ushanka, slapping the sides of his face.

"Your family relocated?"

His child-like eyes stared at the ground.

"Magadan is the city of the dead. There's no going back from here."

First they had been loaded onto a train crammed with hundreds of other citizens and prisoners who were being relocated for the development of the motherland. Siberia, the frozen land, a hidden jewel of future development which would launch Russia into a new sphere of economic development. After a week, the frozen train cars finally came to a halt at a small port town. From there, they were loaded onto ships for their final voyage north to the frozen wasteland to begin their new life.

There were no houses, no definite roads, no railway, and no future.

"I'm Misha."

"Valery Nikolaiavich Nikitin."

They shook hands as Valery shoved the last of the bread in his mouth.

"Why did they send you here?"

"I don't know," he shrugged his shoulders.

"What does your father do?"

"He was an accountant."

"There is no work for an accountant in Siberia, I can tell you that much."

A column of people spilled out of the ship in the harbour and began to form into rows of five. "Where are they taking them?"

"To a camp. They will be forced to work in the mines...if they survive the winter."

Valery looked up from the table, swallowed his vodka and set the glass down. "You've changed, Mikhail." He observed how fat the man had become.

"It comes with age." There was a pause as Misha stared at Valery in silence. "Brother, what have you become? Why did you abandon me?"

"You know as well as I that it was the only way out."

"Was it?" Misha spread his arms. "I sit before you."

"And you, too, have paid a hefty price for your freedom."

Misha buttoned his shirt. "Your woman, what did she tell you?"

"How do you know about Katya?"

The glasses filled with more vodka. "Because I sent her to you." He held out a glass to Valery, who glared at it suspiciously.

"You lie."

"Believe what you must, if it makes you feel better."

Fingers gripped the arms of the chair in silent protest. "Why are you telling me this?"

"I'm wondering, brother, what would it take to make you crack? How do you justify all the people you've killed? Tortured.

How is it that you were so blind as to what was hidden in plain sight?" Misha paused, his eyes locking onto Valery's. "Is it possible that there is still a heart somewhere in there? Did you love her?"

Sunlight reflected off of Katya's hair, giving it a golden sheen as it danced in the wind where she stood on the bridge, throwing bread crumbs to the ducks in the pond. Valery took pleasure watching her from across the park as he approached. As if she could sense him, she looked up, her face brightening as she waved. She threw her arms around his neck, kissing him.

"Dear sweet, Val, you look so glum today."

He set her down. "Not at all, I am happy to see you."

"You should smile more, you act like you're in a prison." She slipped her arm around his and they began walking through the park.

"I've been thinking, Katya, we should get married."

"You know I can't marry you. At least, not until I'm finished school."

"It's only one more year, why wait?"

Katya dropped his arm. "My uncle would never allow it."

"I could protect you, Katyusha." Valery brushed the hair off her face and held her chin.

Valery blinked, his eyes re-focusing on Mikhail. "I lost the last of my humanity years ago."

"Yes…you did, didn't you?" Mikhail's brows turned solemn, creasing his forehead.

A fire burned within the barrel in the corner of the warehouse. Five teenage boys stood huddled around its licking flames for warmth. The side door opened and slammed shut announcing the arrival of Anton and his crew of thieves. They were men in their forties, hardened after a number of years in Siberia and full of vengeance against a corrupt government, on the hunt for retribution for their years of suffering and dreams lost.

Anton slammed a bottle of vodka down on a crate. "Look, I have brought God's tears for us to drink and drown our own sorrows." The other young boys crowded around him, taking turns sipping from the bottle, leaving one boy alone, huddled next to the warmth of the flames. Anton raised his eyebrow as he caught site of the boy. "You! I don't know you. What is your name?"

"Valery Nikolaiavich Nikitin."

"Valery? You are what, twelve, thirteen?"

He nodded coyly.

"Where are your parents?"

Valery looked to his new friend across the room, Alexei downed a shot of vodka, watching the interaction. Anton stepped in his line of sight causing him to look up. "My father was sent to join the war."

"And your mother?"

"Dead."

"You are all alone, little wolf. Well...anyone is welcome to join our pack for a price, of course."

"Price?"

"Alexei did not tell you?"

Valery shook his head. "What is the price?"

Alexei came to stand behind Anton, holding a lead pipe in his hand. Anton gently slid his arm around Valery's shoulders. "You see, Alexei is paying his admission right now. A life, for a life."

A jolt of pain shot through Valery's chest as it tightened. A lump lodged in his throat.

"But I'll tell you what, my lonesome wolf, I will make a deal with you. If you survive, you may take Alexei's place instead."

As Anton stepped back Alexei swung the pipe into Valery's shoulder, knocking him to the ground. There was a flash of light before his eyes, suddenly transporting him back in time. He was three years old and his father was drunk, a huge looming figure standing over his mama in the middle of the living room, his fist raised as he continued to swing punch after punch into his mama's chest. Her screams and wails echoed through Val's ears as he launched himself onto his papa's back, his tiny fists smacking helplessly against his back, tears streaming down his face. "Stop, Papa! Stop!"

His father reached back, grabbed his arm and threw him across the floor. A burning sensation rose up in Valery's feet, coursing up his body and he found himself launching himself across the room at his father again, this time with a kitchen knife in hand. The bellows if his Papa's laughter fueling his anger.

"Niki, no!" his Mama screamed as he pushed a chair in front of Valery, tripping him forward into his mother's arms.

The warmth of his Mama's arms holding him extinguished the adrenaline rush, his anger abating. The warmth continued to spread down his torso as her arms relaxed. The pounding of his heart began to abate from his ears as he looked up into his mother's wide-open glassy eyes.

From behind him, Valery could hear his father gasp. "What have you done?"

Valery blinked again as Alexei gasped, the lead piped clanged against the floor and rolled away. A gurgling rose up from Alexei's throat followed by a red foam of blood. Valery pulled the knife from his chest and the body fell with a thud to the floor.

"Ryumin is being arrested...tonight. He is being investigated for the accusations he made against some Jewish doctors. I believe you were acquainted with one of them, Yakov Etinger." Misha looked up at Valery from over the rim of his class before setting it down.

Valery met Misha's eyes, "Can't say I am."

"It is disheartening to hear that you can torture a man and not even grant him the courtesy of remembering his name."

"It is none of my business what choices other people make."

"Fair enough. What about the choices you have made, brother?"

"Choices? What choices? To live, that is my only choice."

"To live in fear?"

"I have no fear, I deserve whatever punishment God brings me. You think I enjoy what I do?" Valery leaned forward onto the table.

"I think that if we don't put a stop to it, our country will continue to fester in the dark ages."

"Stalin brought this country out of the dark ages."

"Stalin is paranoid and ruthless! The country is beginning to fall apart, Val, and you know it. How much longer do you think we can all go on like this? The fear, paranoia. Murder." Misha took in a deep breath and let it out slowly, his finger tapping the side of his glass.

60

"Do you know how the Vory have managed to survive and grow so strong over the years? I will tell you, Valya. Trust."

"Trust?"

"Trust. It is that simple. We are a family. *You* are a part of this family. You have always been a brother to me, Val. We have a bond so strong. Trust, Valery, that is the nail that binds us together."

"Hmm." Valery drained the vodka from his glass, the cool liquid tracing a trail down his throat until finally warming his stomach.

Misha poured him another glass. "This monster you have become, I know this is not you. This is not the boy I met twenty years ago."

Chapter Eight

"You are young to be sent to a work camp, no?" Misha commented as they walked down the frozen road. "Where is your family now?"

"They are dead."

"In the Gulag?"

"No, my father died last winter. He was drunk and passed out in the snow. Froze to death."

"And your mother?"

The boy hesitated a moment before answering. "She died a long time ago."

Mikhail put his arm around Valery's shoulders. "I am sorry. To lose your mother so young, that is a terrible fate. Do you have any siblings?"

"No."

Misha stopped, two pools of piercing blue looking deep into Valery's eyes. "Then I will be your brother, Valya. I will always look out for you. I promise." A faint smile passed over his lips, his eyes brightening as his hands squeezed Valery's shoulders. Valery had no reason to trust him, but for some reason, he did. "We are in Siberia now, but I promise you one day we'll take our country back. We will make our Mother proud."

Misha inhaled deep, letting his breath out slow as he eyes looked over Valery. His lips pursed before finally speaking. "I never told you this, but you used to cry in your sleep. I never said anything, I didn't want to embarrass you."

Valery's cold gaze gave way as an eyebrow twitched.

"The first time I saw the scars across your back, it took everything I had not to cry for you. You had this wall built up around you. You still do, Valya. But you are my brother, and I swore to protect you no matter what." Misha leaned forward, clasping his hands on the table, his thumb gently rubbing over the knuckle of the other. "You need to release the past, Valya. Release the stranglehold it has on you, it is the only way you will be free."

"There is nothing to release."

"I need you to come home, Valya. Come home, brother. Help me make Mother proud." Misha paused, waiting for Valery's eyes to meet his. "Tell me how this monster was created. Tell me…what did they do to you?"

"I don't know what you mean?" Valery began to slowly turn his glass on the table.

"In Lipetsk…the Germans. What did they do to you?"

There was a loud explosion and the building at the end of the street broke apart. The top corner crumbled to the street exposing the small naked apartment within. Valery ran screaming down the alley, the pop of gunfire erupting behind him. Pieces of brick spat out from the wall where the bullets hit. His feet tripped on a pile of rubble and he fell, skinning his hands where he landed. A warm sensation crawled up his arm and he could feel the pounding of blood fill his bruised palm. He knew it was forbidden to enter the wasted remains of the old city quarter, destroyed from the war and now used by the military for training.

A click of a machine gun being loaded caused his spine to tense. He remained frozen where he was, praying that if he could just keep still long enough, no one would see him. A black boot stepped up beside him.

"What have we here?"

"Some kind of small Russian rat, Commander."

"Indeed.

They were German soldiers, but they spoke Russian well enough to be understood. Valery began to shake uncontrollably as he stared at the ground in front of him. A piece of brick dug deeper into his hand.

"Perhaps we should show him some good German hospitality?" The men laughed.

Something hard struck Valery in the back of his head and his vision went black.

When he awoke, he lay naked on a small bed, his wrists tied to the frame. One of the German solders sat nearby smoking a cigarette. In another room muffled screams from another child.

"Don't worry yourself, boy. They are just playing." The soldier inhaled from his cigarette deep and then slowly let the smoke snake out of his mouth. "Shall we play? I know a fun game." He held the cigarette between his fingers, studying it a moment before looking at Valery. He blew gently at the end of the cigarette, causing it to turn red. "I think it's time for you to learn how powerful the German Reich is. This game is called 'if you scream, I'll kill you'."

Out of the corner of his eye Valery could see his hand hover over his body. His torso jerked suddenly as the pain of a thousand bee stings hit him, and then subsided into numbness. The German laughed to himself before repeating the act on one of Valery's nipples. Valery squeezed his eyes shut, his jaw clenched as tears streamed down his face.

The torture went on for hours, his body covered in sores. He came in and out of consciousness as visions of his babushka's dacha on a warm summer's day drifted in and out of his thoughts. The smile on his mother's face as she took him into the orchard always made him smile in return.

"Valya, come, help me pick apples from the tree." She tied her scarf tight over her head to keep her hair in place and handed him a small basket. Gently she took his hand in hers and led him over to the tree where she had already laid out a blanket on the grass.

The sun would peak through the branches from above as his mama hummed to herself, plucking apples from the tree. Valya would toss any that fell into his own basket while munching on another in his other hand. Suddenly a large apple fell from above and hit him on his head and he couldn't stop himself from crying.

"It will all be over soon. Quiet, you're a big boy now." The voice was not soft and sweet, but gruff and full of menace.

Valery opened his eyes, his face smooshed into a pillow. His body numb from the neck down. The soldier grabbed his neck from behind, pushing his face further into the bed as he leaned into his ear. "Pretty soon, we'll make men out of you all."

As he screamed his mother picked him up, holding him tightly in her arms. "Shhh, my little Valya. Mama has you now."

There was darkness and silence for a long time. The faint sounds of boots in the distance somewhere outside.

Valery gasped and tried to open his eyes but something sticky kept them shut. His body began to shiver, which only caused him to become conscious of the pain. There was no one spot which hurt more than another, rather, his entire body hurt. Even the cool air on his skin hurt.

Time ceased to exist the longer he lay there. Reality ceased to exist. Maybe he was already dead?

There was a faint smell of smoke wafting in through an open window, the glass shattered from an explosion. The floor creaked and the door knob could be heard gently hitting the wall behind it. And then there were screams.

"I don't know how long I was in hospital." Valery grabbed the bottle of vodka and poured himself a drink, knocking it back quickly before pouring another.

Misha watched him carefully, his breaths deep and long. "They were the monsters, Valya. The German soldiers."

"It doesn't matter now, Misha."

"It does matter! Look at you. Look what you allowed them to create, in you. You are not this monster, Valya."

"I don't feel angry anymore. I'm not angry about what happened to me. I feel nothing."

Mikhail slid his hand forward on the table towards Valery, their fingers just touching. "It's not your fault. You did not deserve to have such a fate. You should not be embarrassed or ashamed."

Valery jerked his hand away. "I told you. I feel nothing." He poured the shot of vodka down his throat, the glass cool in his hand.

"What about Katya?" Misha paused, watching for some kind of reaction on Valery's face. "Did you love her?"

"Katya betrayed me." Valery's hand gripped the arm rest on his chair.

"Did you love her?"

The shot glass shattered against the far wall as Valery rose and walked to the window. He crossed his arms and stared through the

66

curtain into the night. "Why have you brought me here, Misha? It can't be to just reminisce about the past."

Mikhail stood, his frame taking on that of a great bear. "Answer me! Did you love her?"

Valery gave Misha a quick glance out of the corner of his eye before returning his reflection in the window. "I thought I did."

Misha stepped closer. "We're going to take back our country, Valya. You and I, together." He placed a hand on each shoulder, looking Valery in the face. "Come, I have something to show you."

Mikhail's arm draped around Valery's shoulder as they walked across the room to a window which overlooked the courtyard below. Drawing back the curtain, Valery gazed at the large white flakes drifting to the ground. Efim was leaning against the car, catching sight of the men in the window he jumped to attention, threw his cigarette on the ground, and then quickly opened the rear door of the car.

A dainty foot stepped out followed by the small frame of a woman in a black wool coat with a grey scarf. She shoved her hands in her pockets as Efim closed the door behind her, and then led her into the warm golden light of the hotel.

Valery's hand lay plastered against the cold glass, his face nearly pressed up against it. Finally he let out his breath, fogging the view he had. He squeezed his eyes shut, dipping his head, his shoulders rose as he inhaled like a bear catching the scent of its prey. "She's alive?"

"She is."

"She deceived me." The words ground between Valery's teeth.

"No, she only did what I told her to do."

"It was all a lie." Valery glanced up at Misha. "This was all a plot to get to me."

Mikhail motioned for Valery to sit down again at the table. "That part is true, yes. But she does love you, Valya. She didn't do it to hurt you."

With his lower back resting against the windowsill and arms crossed over his chest, Valery stared at Mikhail in silence. "Why?"

"Why, Valya? Why did you really come to Moscow?" Mikhail turned Valery from across the room.

Silence filled the room as the seconds swept by like minutes, forgotten, before Valery could bring himself to look at Mikhail again. "The same reason everyone dreams of but never speaks about."

Part Three

The Authority

Chapter Nine

The doorknob turned and the door swung open. A thin scrawny man stepped aside to reveal the angelic figure of Katya; she stepped into the room and the door closed behind her. Her eyes shifted nervously over to Misha. Mikhail stepped up to her and kissed her cheeks as he placed a reassuring hand on her shoulder. "I will be just outside."

The door closed leaving Katya and Valery in silence. He turned away from her, choosing only to watch her reflection in the window. They both stood in silence, neither brave enough to make a move.

"I'm sorry." Her voice was barely a whisper.

Valery remained transfixed on her reflection. "It was all a lie."

Katya took a step forward. "No. Not all of it."

Valery stared at his own reflection when he spoke. "They told me you were dead."

"It was the only way we'd know for sure..."

He turned around, his eyes bearing down on her. "Know what?"

"The truth." Her lip trembled as she spoke.

"What truth is that, Katya? That I am a monster."

"No."

He lunged forward, crossing the room swiftly to stand towering over her. His lips brushed against her ear as he spoke. "I saw the way you looked at me in there. All you saw was the monster. The man who you thought you knew didn't exist. He never existed, Katya. He was a dream."

Katya steadied her nerves as she pulled back to look at him. "You're wrong, he does exist. I'm looking at him now."

Valery stepped over to the table and poured himself another shot of vodka, quickly slamming it back before he focused his eyes back on Katya. "So, he's your father?"

"Yes." She rubbed her hands nervously. "Not my real father, he adopted me."

"Well then we are related. Misha adopted me when I was a boy, sent to the Gulag in Siberia." He settled himself back into a chair still holding the empty shot glass in his hand. "What happened to your real family?"

Katya coyly stepped forward and slid herself into the chair opposite him. Her eyes remained glued to the table. "I don't know. The Gulag maybe. Maybe dead." She paused, her fingers reaching up to play with her scarf. "I came home from school one day and they were gone. They never returned."

Valery grunted and slouched down in his chair. "Why am I here, Katya? What does he want?"

Slowly she raised her eyes up to his face. "You're the only person he trusts. There is so much turmoil going on in the country. The Communist party is falling apart. He wants to make his move in the Vory. And to do that he wants you as his Obshchak."

Valery scoffed, but couldn't help but consider the offer. He would be second. He would no longer be beholden to an unpredictable regime. The Vory were the order within the chaos of the country.

His fingers turned the smooth shot glass in his hand. "He sends a woman to do his begging for him."

"No, he doesn't know that I am telling you this. But I do because…I need to make things right between us. No more lies, Valya."

He looked up and met her eyes, giving her a slight nod. "What is your part in all this?"

"I don't have one. He wanted you back, that's all."

"This is not the life for a woman. What will you do?"

"I will return to school and finish my degree."

"Right, economics. It all makes sense now. He plans to infiltrate from within the government."

Katya's eyes darted to the window, then the bottle of vodka, and finally back to Valery. As she opened her mouth to speak he placed the shot glass back on the table, knocking it against the wood, and poured another shot. Slowly he pushed it across the table to her.

"There is no need to explain yourself. You're a smart girl, Kat. Drink, we are going to be family."

"You will do this?"

"I will do this. But not because of you Katya, and not because I owe my life to Misha. This, I do for me."

Katya got up and went towards the door, she paused a moment as she placed her hand on the doorknob.

"Kat…if I do this, there's no coming back." He meant that in more ways than one. There would be no coming back to her. And no coming back from the monster he was about to unleash. And no coming back from whatever Misha had in store as punishment for him.

Still facing the door, she gave a slight nod, then opened the door and slipped out. Misha watched as she walked past, giving him a slight nod before disappearing down the hallway. He pushed open the door and stepped back into the room. "She told you?"

Valery reached across the table, grabbing the shot he had poured for Katya. "What is my punishment, Misha? What is it you want me to do?"

Misha closed the door and sat at the table. He inhaled and exhaled slowly before replying. "I need you to send a message to the Vory."

"A message?" Valery cocked an eyebrow. "What kind of message?"

"I need you to kill Vladislav Malyshev."

Valery eyed Misha in silence. He lifted the shot glass to his mouth and slowly tipped it back, letting the cool liquid slide down his throat. "That's more than just a message. That's a decree."

"I suppose it is. He will be at the Yelokhovo Cathedral tomorrow at midnight, every Wednesday without fail. You can do it then."

"We don't spill blood on holy ground."

"Inside, outside, do it however you want. You became a Suka when you left, Val. It was only because of me and your reputation that you were left alone. Do this for me and you'll be my Avtoritet. Once you prove yourself, I will make you Obshchak."

Valery tapped a finger on the table in the silence as he considered Misha's order. "The State Security will be looking for the killer, it may crush your ascension."

Misha's eyes twitched up, seeming to enjoy what he was about to say. "You will allow them to arrest you. They'll send you to the White Swan because they know it's the only place that could contain you. There you will put word out to the Vory that I am in charge. They won't argue with you."

Valery's finger went still. He had spent years trying to silence the memories which haunted his dreams of his time there. But if he refused, Misha would probably kill him where he sat. "And then?"

"I have contacts there." He leaned forward, resting his elbows on the table. "Don't worry, I'll get you out. I don't take pleasure in this, Valya. You have always been like a real son to me, I know how this place broke you."

"Broke me?" Valery rose to his feet, towering over Mikhail. For a brief moment fear and panic flashed across Misha's face.

"It unleashed this beast in you, Valya. The one you had been suppressing since you were a boy. This beast that never sleeps. I am giving you the opportunity to reconcile with it. I need you by my side, and I need to know that you will never try to stray again."

"I have nowhere else to go. This is who I am. I obey only you, Pakhan."

Misha stood and held out his arm, waiting for Valery to clasp his. A smile creased his lips. "And to prove that all is forgiven, let's get you inked." He called in two men from the hall who entered the room carrying small wooden boxes full of tools for tattooing.

Valery removed his shirt, revealing his tattooed and scarred body. Stars on his shoulders, denoting his previous rank and authority in the Zone. A rose and dagger along his ribs, how he spent is eighteenth birthday in prison. The dagger through his neck dripping with blood symbolizing all the people he had murdered. A double headed eagle with a Madonna and child on his back, above them written *The Land of Slaves*. On his other rib, a swan dripping is blood, symbolizing his first stay at the White Swan prison.

And tonight, he would get two epaulettes, one on each shoulder emblazoned with three stars to denote his new rank as

Avtoritet. A second head to his swan, to denote his intended second incarceration there. And then finally, a new ring on the middle finger of his right hand, a crown and dagger to represent the murder of a Vladislav Malyshev, the current Krestniy Otets.

Chapter Ten

Misha handed Valery a gun as he stepped out of the car. "You make me proud, Valya." The door closed and the car drove away, disappearing around the corner of a building. Valery shoved the gun in his pocket and entered his apartment building.

Each step up to his apartment creaked and groaned under his weight, as if his victims pleaded with him to stop the madness. But the beast ignored them, the soles of his shoes scraping the worn wood beneath them.

His apartment was cold, each breath appearing in a small cloud of vapour before his face. He lit a fire in the kitchen stove before finally wandering into the bedroom. He sat down on the bed, his body slouched over, the gun in his pocket digging into his hip. He placed it on the table beside the bed and lay back, as his head hit the pillow Katya's scent drifted into his nostrils. The dream of a normal life vanishing with each breath.

A small knock on the door stirred him from slumber, a small ray of sunlight slicing across the room as he tried to open his eyes. Was it all a bad dream? As he sat up he saw the gun next to him, he shoved it back into his pocket as he stood. The knocking on his door grew persistent.

His boots felt heavy on his feet, each step thundering across the floor. Finally, he unlocked the door and opened it. Katya's tired face gazed up at him, her cheeks pink from the cold. "Can I come in?"

He stepped away, heading back to the kitchen stove. He opened its small door and poked at the embers inside, stirring them back to life as he added more wood. Somewhere across the apartment he heard the front door close and Katya's delicate footsteps approach him. He pulled a chair up next to the stove and sat down, slouching in it as he crossed his arms over his chest.

"What are you doing here, Katya?"

She stood in the doorway watching him nervously. "I came to see if you were all right."

He cocked an eyebrow, his gaze remaining fixed on the flickering new flames in the stove.

"I'm sorry." Her voice trembled, sounding small.

"You shouldn't be here." He grit the words out between clenched teeth.

Her response was barely a whisper under her breath. "I know." Tentatively she stepped closer to the stove to warm her hands. "I had no idea who you were when we first met, all I knew was that you used to work for Misha and he wanted you back. Had I known, maybe I wouldn't have been so naïve. But I want you to know, that is the man I fell in love with."

Valery inhaled long and deep and then slowly exhaled; his gaze remained fixed on the stove.

"And even after the first time we made love and I got a glimpse of some of your tattoos under your clothing… I knew why you refused to take them off, you thought it would frighten me away. But it was already too late, Valya, I was in love with you and I didn't care." She wiped a stray tear from her cheek with her gloved hand. "There is a good man inside you, I've seen him. And I know you don't have a choice in what you have to do. But I just wanted you to know that, I will always love you, Val."

She inhaled the wet sniffle in her nose, waiting for some kind of response from him. His stoic demeanor remained frozen where he sat. "Goodbye, Valya," she whispered as she turned and walked out of the room.

"Kat." His gruff voice seemed to reach out, causing her feet to stick to the floor. Her body trembled. She could hear him stand and his heavy footfalls as he came up behind her. The floor shaking with each step until he stopped behind her. "I won't be returning after tomorrow. Don't look for me. Forget about me. You need a man who can take care of you. Live your life. A good life. But the man you knew is already dead."

Her breath stuck in her throat, stifling her cries as she walked out of his apartment. The pain in her chest felt like he had ripped her heart out and throw it into the fire, watching it burn. An image of him standing over her at the prison flashed through her mind. The image of the beast who never slept – only it did sleep. All those months together, the beast had slept.

She had tamed the beast.

And now she was responsible for reawakening it. Katya ran down the street trying to get away from him as fast as she could. Trying to run away from the tears which were freezing to her cheeks. Trying to run from the broken pieces of her heart which throbbed in her chest.

Valery watched from his apartment window as Katya disappear down the street. Now nothing but a faded memory. A dream which disappeared in the blinding glow of the sunlight as it reflected off the snow on the street.

He glanced around his apartment wondering if there was anything he should do before he left that evening. Was there anything he needed stored somewhere safe? Was there anyone he needed to say goodbye to?

There was nothing. No one.

The only person who used to matter, had just left.

Fresh snow drifted from the dark clouds overhead, Valery shoved his gloved hands deeper into his pockets. The Yelokhovo Cathedral stood vigilant in the cold night. The golden domes were covered with a light coating of snow. The heels of Valery's boots crunched loudly as he crossed the small plaza to the honey coloured wooden doors snuggled at the base of the aqua blue and white painted exterior of the cathedral. All religion had been banned by the Communist Party, and yet it still remained at the heart of the Russian Empire no matter how hard they tried to rip it out.

As he opened the door a rush of warm air seized him and seemed to pull him inside. His hand clenched the gun in his pocket. He stepped forward, admiring all the gold and frescoes on the walls which glowed amber in the candlelight. His heart kept a steady rhythm as he watched Vladislav Malyshev kneeling at the altar.

Patiently he waited for the man to stand. From behind he appeared short, but broad shouldered. His form shrouded and weighted down by his black wool coat. When he turned around his feet paused as his eyes met Valery's across the room. Gathering his courage, Vladislav began to slowly step forward. Valery matched him step for step until they were a short distance from each other in the middle of the cathedral.

"So, the beast who never sleeps has finally emerged from hibernation. I heard you've been working for the butcher, Ryumin."

"I was."

Malyshev's eyes widened as he raised his eyebrows, intrigued by Valery's blatant admission. "You want back into the Vory then, is that why you are here? You know I can't allow that, you are a Suka. Even I can't protect you." He laughed at the idea of Valery being beaten and harassed by other Vory. The same men who feared him.

Valery's hand clenched the gun in his pocket. "No, I am already back in. Once a Vor, always a Vor. I'm only here to deliver a message." His hand slid out of his jacket pocket holding the gun pointed directly at Vladislav.

"Do not spill blood in the house of the Lord!" The words echoed from the priest standing at the altar. The man blended in so well with the interior that Valery had missed seeing him.

His eyes shifted from the priest back to Malyshev. "Not my house." The leather of his glove creaked as his finger put pressure on the trigger of the gun. With a sudden jolt the gun exploded.

Malyshev stumbled back, his hand pressed against this chest. A wet patch began to appear, the dark liquid smearing his hand. His knees weakened and he stumbled to the floor. Trying desperately to hold himself he leaned on a pew, leaving behind a smear of blackened blood as his body fell to the floor.

The priest ran from the altar, exiting through a rear door. Valery settled himself into a nearby pew, the gun ground against the wooden bench as he slid it next to him. His eyes gazed up at the religious motifs surrounding him. He basked in the warm glow which reflected from all the gold adorning the walls and ceiling, surprised that the Communist Party had yet to confiscate it.

Calmly he waited. The minutes dragged on in the silence until finally he could hear vehicles outside and the commotion of the security officers preparing to enter the cathedral. Patiently he waited for them, listening to their tentative footsteps as they made their way down the Nave towards him.

"Citizen, do not move," one of them commanded.

Out of the corner of his eye Valery could see two officers stop next to the body on the floor. "That's Malyshev," one of them quietly told the other from where he knelt. When he glanced up at Valery he froze, nearly falling to the floor. His entire body began to shake as he tried to stand, his eyes frozen on the gun next to Valery. "C…C…Comrade Nikitin, we need you to come with us."

Valery turned to the man, eyeing him as a man would a bug on the wall. He stood and adjusted his jacket before turning to face the officers. Carefully he stepped over the body and the pool of black liquid which had collected around it. The officers shuffled back, pointing their guns tepidly towards Valery. "Of course." He motioned with his hand for them to lead the way.

From where he sat in the back of the car Valery could sense the fear of the two officers in the front seat, each nervously checking the rear-view mirror to make sure that he was still in the back seat. Stoically Val looked out the window at the buildings passing by. He already knew his fate, and he was at peace with it.

The car stopped outside Lubyanka and the officers walked him inside the prison. They led him down a dark hall meant to invoke fear into the criminals brought there. But for Valery it was home. He settled into the small wooden chair in what they used as an "intimidation room" for questioning. Little questioning every happened in one. The door closed and the lock clicked, leaving nothing but the sounds of the officers' boots disappearing down the hall.

Valery inhaled deep, stretching out his long legs where he sat. Leaning back he eyed the small singular yellow bulb of light hanging above his head. His gaze fell to the small hole in the center of the floor next to his feet.

He had memories of this place. Indifferent memories. Dreamlike remembrances. A hazy fog of recollections when the monster inside him would be let loose. That was why they had sent him to Sukhanovka. They could not contain the monster within him, but they could hide him away in a dark basement where he could be unleashed and hidden from those with a more delicate constitution. But it could not stop the rumors.

How was it possible for one man to be capable of such horrific acts?

So calm on the outside, a quiet man who kept to himself. No sense of anger or rage could be found. But once behind closed doors the monster which lurked deep within would be released, doing what it was commanded to do in the name of the Communist Party to protect the Motherland.

But now the beast had a new mission.

Chapter Eleven

Valery sat with his arms crossed across his chest, body slouched in the chair, legs extended in front of him when the door finally opened. Minister Abakumov stepped inside followed by two more officers. The door closed and they all stood staring at Valery, at the ready if he tried anything and they needed to escape.

"I would congratulate you for doing us a favour for killing Malyshev, but I'm not sure why you did it. Were you told to do it, Comrade Nikitin?"

He remained apathetic. "I was."

The tension in Abakumov's body began to recede. "I knew you must have been given an order. But in a church?" He laughed. "You really are a Communist, aren't you?"

Valery remained silent, staring calmly at the Minister.

"You're reputation precedes you, the officers were too terrified to cuff you I see."

Valery looked down at his crossed arms and then back to Abakumov.

"I need you to tell me who ordered you to kill Vladislav Malyshev."

"You'll know soon enough."

Abakumov glanced back at the two officers behind him nervously. "Did this come from Ryumin?"

"No."

"It didn't come from my office, where did it come from?"

"Did you really think you would be able to keep me caged up in that basement out at Sukhanovka forever? Did you really think the Vory wouldn't come looking for me?"

Abakumov's hand slid to the gun on his hip, the two officers behind him following suit. "You know we can't let this go unpunished. We have to send a message to anyone else who thinks they can just go around killing people."

"In churches," Valery added. "Of course."

Valery's insolence fueled Abakumov's anger. "We'll have to send you to the White Swan."

"I expect you will." Valery's lack of emotion, lack of guilt for what he had just done, and lack of fear for where he was being sent, left Abakumov uncomfortable. The two officers stepped forward and waited for Valery to stand.

"Why did you do it, Comrade Nikitin?"

Valery's eyes met Minister Abakumov's, he could see the man's curiosity. "I am the monster who never sleeps. Pray, Minister, that we never meet again."

One of the officers pulled a set of cuffs from his pocket, the metal clinking tauntingly. A smirk rose up on the corner of the man's mouth, quickly fading as Valery began to pull the gloves from his hands, revealing the new ring tattooed on his middle finger symbolizing the murder of a Vor boss. After shoving his gloves in his pockets he turned around and placed his arms behind his back for them.

A short time later Valery boarded a train to Kazan. The cold and noise made it nearly impossible to sleep. As the morning sun rose it cast its warmth across his face like a warm hand, bringing with it memories of Katya. He opened his eyes, banishing the thoughts as he stared out at the bleak landscape, frozen, cold, and devoid of emotion.

Once in Kazan, he was transferred to a truck. A handful of prison guards accompanied him, their faces hardened by years of prison service. Valery's face once looked like that, a mask hiding the fear within. In Russia, everyone wore a mask. Valery's mask kept him alive even after he had gone against the Vory and become a prison guard in exchange for more freedoms in the Gulag. He was not meant to be caged like an animal. The longer he was caged, the more the monster within him crawled to the surface.

Over time Valery's boyhood fears were replaced by stoic indifference. A face that did not care whether it lived or died.

At the prison he was taken into the showers and ordered to strip. He did as he was told, placing his clothing neatly on the bench against the wall. The prison guards begin to chatter at the sight of the fresh tattoos on his shoulders and ribs. Valery cast them a glance from under his heavy brows, daring them to challenge his new authority.

Naked and helpless, they intimidate, humiliate, and instill fear by way of a cold shower. To cause physical anguish, literally freezing the prisoner in the dead of winter. Valery's hulking frame stood in the shower room waiting for the water to be turned on. The tattoos on his body lay bare for all the prison guards to read the story about the legendary beast who never slept.

The voices feel quiet, eyes darting back and forth among each other before someone finally spoke, "Get dressed."

The guards stepped outside the door, waiting for Valery to put his clothes back on and join them.

He was marched through the halls, a prized catch being taken to the prison Commander's office. When the door opened, Valery recognized the man's face immediately. The Kazakh. No one knew what his real name was. The man looked up from the papers on his desk, he set his cigarette in the ashtray and then stood.

The Kazakh looked even older than Valery remembered. Short and fat, he had a pockmarked face which he tried to hide with a beard. Warm and endearing on the outside like a wolverine, he also had the ability rip into minds and bodies with sadistic delight.

"This one is barely a man, Gosha. What could this boy have done to deserve the safety of being under my roof?"

Gosha laughed as he held Valery's skinny arm. "They say he's a Vor, Commander."

"A Vor?" He eyed the anger of Valery's boyish face. "So angry, boy. Press him."

"Yes, sir."

Immediately he was taken back into the heart of the White Swan's cold dark hallways. The floors wet and muddy from the spring rains. Another guard unlocked a heavy metal door revealing a small room with four bunkbeds crammed with close to thirty prisoners like a can of sardines.

A sharp pain clenched Valery's chest as he looked at the hardened criminals staring back at him. Their bodies thin, almost frail, and covered with tattoos and scars. Their heads had been shaved to help prevent the spread of disease and lice.

"Don't be afraid boy, these are your kind. I could have put in with the priests, they like young boys." The guard laughed as he shoved Valery inside, the door clanging shut and locking behind him.

Valery scanned the cell, his now hulking stature enveloping the door frame as he stepped inside. The chatter from the inmates became hushed as his eyes observed the crowded room. He took step forward and the door slammed shut behind him, the lock grinding into place.

A skinny man dressed in tattered clothing pushed his way through the overcrowded room and stood before him; he recognized him immediately.

"Well, if it isn't little Valya, all grown up. We heard you became a Suka. Suka's don't last very long here." His eyes peered out like small black dots on his face.

Valery calmly began to remove his leather gloves from his hands, finger by finger, pulling them loose.

"So quiet, Valya. Nothing to say?"

Ignoring the man, Valery shoved the gloves in his pockets. As he raised his hands up to the buttons on his jacket a few gasps escaped the cluster of onlookers. "Sasha!" one of the men hissed, trying to alert his Comrade.

"What? I do not trust a man who doesn't speak. Is he deaf now? Dumb?" Sasha continued to jeer.

"His hand," someone else mumbled.

Sasha's eyes focused on the hands which deftly began to pull the jacket from Valery's body, which he handed to a young man next to him who stood frozen in awe of the giant before him undressing.

But Sasha was looking for a fight, as a Lieutenant in the Vory, he needed to maintain his rank in the prison, but when Valery pulled the sweater over his head his complexion paled. Valery's gaze met every man's in the room before he finally spoke. "Vladislav Malyshev is dead. Mikhail Sokolov is now Pakhan."

"How did he die?" someone asked from within the crowd.

"I shot him…in a church," Valery said as he pulled his sweater back on and grabbed his coat from the shaking arms of the man beside him.

"We heard you were working for Stalin," Sasha said. "Deserted us. Doing the dirty work for the state."

"I was," Valery answered as he pulled his gloves back on.

"How do we know you are telling the truth?"

Valery began to step forward, the men pushing against themselves to allow him through. "Ask the guards." He stopped once he found a chair against the wall and sat down.

Sasha followed him. "And now you are here, stuck inside the Swan while Misha is free." He began to laugh. "He set you up, Valya."

"He did." Valery's stony gaze rose up to Sasha.

Sasha's laughter faded.

"He's hoping that you will take swift care of me, do his dirty work for him. Well, I am here now. So if you think you can, do it."

Reaching behind his back, Sasha pulled a sharpened piece of metal and held it before Valery's face.

"Sasha!" someone else hissed at him from the crowd of onlookers. "Put it down."

Valery leaned back in the chair, resting an elbow on the small rickety table beside him, the other hand on his lap. "Now is your chance. Don't miss, Sasha."

The knuckles on Sasha's hand began to turn white as he gripped the shank tighter. Bending his knees, he got himself into position to lunge forward. His eyes narrowed and the smirk on his face lengthened. Valery knew Sasha had no choice but to do it, as a Lieutenant, he had to maintain his dominance and control at all cost. Even the cost of his own life.

Sasha lunged forward taking aim at Valery's neck. In one swift, fluid motion, Valery grabbed Sasha's arm while the other hand knocked the knife around and together they plunged it into soft flesh under Sasha's chin.

Blood bubbled out of the wound as Sasha gurgled, trying to breathe. Valery released him and he fell to the floor at his feet. Sasha looked up at him, almost thankful to no longer have to live. Then finally lay still in the expanding pool of dark liquid creeping across the floor.

Two prisoners grabbed Sasha's feet and dragged him to the door. One pounded on the door with is fist. A guard slid the cover on the small window open, "What do you want?"

"Sasha has killed himself." He stepped back so the guard could see the body.

The guard glanced down. "He killed himself?"

"Yes."

The guard raised an eyebrow, knowing full well the truth. But also knowing, this was a Gulag prison, the White Swan. And these were the Vory. It was their kingdom, and if they say Sasha killed himself. Then, Sasha killed himself.

That first night Valery lay in bed listening to the heavy breathing and snores of the men around him. Hardened men who were once terrified little boys who had been sucked into the underworld of the Vory. For many it was all they knew. The only family they had after losing their own. It was a game of survival. Others had been thrown into the life through no choice of their own, just in the wrong place at the right time.

The next day word began to spread about Malyshev's death and Mikhail Sokolov's rise. But it was the Beast of White Swan who everyone feared.

Breakfast consisted of some type of porridge, Valery was almost certain the dark specks in it were bugs. Two guards stopped him on his way back to his cell, directing him down the all too familiar cramped hallways towards the prison Commander's office. The small stove in the corner of the office was lit, providing what little warmth could be coaxed out of it.

The Kazakh looked up from his papers as the men entered. Valery took a seat in the chair opposite while the two guards stood on either side of him.

"You lost a Comrade yesterday," the Kazakh said as he opened a drawer and pulled out a pack of cigarettes.

Valery glanced towards the window. "Yes, I think he was happy to see me."

The Commander smiled. "You're a funny man. Very funny. I don't remember you having a sense of humour."

He returned his gaze to The Kazakh. "It's been a while."

The smile faded as the Commander sat back in his chair and lit a cigarette, throwing the extinguished match on the floor. "I hear you have some new tattoos."

Valery remained stoic, waiting for the man to speak again.

"You knew you were coming here again, huh? This was planned, this reunion?"

"It was not my plan."

The Commander nodded at the two guards to leave. As the door shut he leaned forward over his desk. "It seems you have friends in high places and you are an asset to the state. Minister Abakumov has made an offer, he would like you to continue your invaluable service to the state."

"You are releasing me?" It took all his effort to keep his voice steady.

The Kazakh laughed, slapping his knee. "I like this humour." His smile faded and he grew serious. "Here." His finger plunged at his desk.

"Here?" Valery was incredulous, but his face remained indifferent. Of course they would force him to do it here. Everyone had a message to send, Valery was a regular carrier pigeon. Only his messages were always dead and covered in blood.

"And if you do well, we may consider transferring you to a less restrictive prison."

By less restrictive, he meant Siberia.

"What's in it for me?" It was a fair question, doing their dirty work made no difference to Valery, he had been doing other people's dirty work for most of his life already.

"Name it, whatever you want. We can get you a girl. A boy if you like, even. Extra rations, cigarettes, vodka."

The two men remained still, each watching the other intently in the silence with only the crackle of wood in the stove to indicate that time was still moving.

"All right," Valery finally said.

The Commander exhaled, his shoulders relaxing. "I'm beginning to think you enjoy it, Comrade Nikitin." His brows softened and his voice lowered. "Perhaps I was too hard on you as a boy."

91

Valery stood in the prison yard watching as two guards tied the prisoner between two wooden posts in the ground. The Kazakh placed his hand on Valery's shoulder, "Go on boy."

His boots slurped in the mud with each step towards the man. He held the knife out in front of him.

"He was the one, yes?"

Valery nodded.

"Then show him what kind of a man you are."

For hours they stood out in the spring sun as Valery used the knife to carve into the soft flesh of the prisoner. Carving out his own tattoos which would leave the man scarred, letting everyone who saw him know what sort of a sick pedophilic rapist he was. Valery left no patch of skin untouched.

After the first thirty minutes the tremor had left his hand. After the first hour, the anger had melted from his heart. After two hours he almost began to feel sorry for the man, watching as he screamed, his body dripping in blood, all colour draining away into the mud at his feet along with every emotion Valery had ever kept hidden deep within himself.

And when he was done he turned around to find that he was alone in the prison yard. What had started out as entertainment amongst jeers and cheering had faded to a circus show, until finally it was nothing more than a beast and his prey left to the wild.

The metal hinges ground open to reveal a thin naked man lying on the dirty cold floor. It was as if Jesus had fallen from the cross before him. His body was frail, the outline of the man's ribs protruded from his chest so much that Valery could tell which had been broken at one time. The strong stench of urine stung the air even though there were only bars on the window and a slight breeze of fresh winter air swept in.

The door slammed shut behind him, leaving the two men alone. Valery stood silent and still, watching for any sort of movement from the man. Perhaps he was already dead?

He was given no information as to why this man was in prison. No source of information which he was to obtain. No charge which had been laid against him. Because he existed, he was here.

"Who are you?" Valery finally asked.

The man's body jerked at the sound his voice.

"What is your name?" he asked, watching for any other signs of life.

Finally the man attempted to open his swollen eyes, his lips trembled as he tried to move his mouth. His voice was a hoarse whisper. "Father Ivanov."

"How long have you been in prison?"

"Six years."

It was only the previous year that the Stoglav Council had been formed in Moscow. Joseph Stalin had come to an agreement with the Orthodox Church to allow limited rights of the church to reopen in Russia.

"Why are you here?"

"I'm...a priest."

"The church has been reinstated," Valery informed the man. "So why are you still here?"

Suddenly the man began to cry, his entire body shaking. "Then, it is over?"

Valery stepped forward and knelt next to the man, placing his hand on the man's head. "No, it's not over."

Chapter Twelve

Valery lay in his bunk as the other men in the room chattered amongst themselves, joking and laughing. It seemed insane that these hardened criminals, many who would live out the rest of their lives behind these walls, would be able to find a sliver of happiness. Grateful only to be alive for one more day.

Each day blended into the next. Prison life became normal again. His new status within the prison offered many perks, better food was the only one that really mattered to Valery.

Every day the guards would take him to an interrogation cell where he would meet with another prisoner, and through whatever means necessary, he would extract information from them. The only ones who required coaxing were the ones who had no idea who he was. Most did not have anything of value to offer in the way of information, many in for petty crimes, opting for time spent in jail with a roof over their head and some food in their belly over starving in the streets.

The Vory were eager to pass on information about Misha's rise to power and the sway he had in Moscow. He boasted about taming The Beast, using Valery's reputation to keep men in check. And then joked that if anyone got sent to the White Swan, to say hi to Valery for him, and remind him what happens to traitors.

But Misha's boasting had no place at the Swan. The Swan was Valery's kingdom now.

The rusted hinges ground open and Valery stepped into the room. Five older men huddling around candles inside, barely paying any notice to him as he made his way over to the man lying on the bunk in the corner of the room.

"I brought you bread and sausage," Valery said as he sat down on the stool next to him.

The man opened his eyes, his frail hands emerging from beneath the tattered blanket to grasp the metal tin Valery held out to him. "Thank you." Valery watched him shift his body to prop his head against the wall so he could eat. Slowly he chewed a bite of sausage and swallowed it before speaking. "It's Christmas today," he finally said. "Thank you for this precious gift. I can't imagine what you had to do to get it."

Valery leaned forward, resting his elbows on his knees, his silence spoke more than he ever could.

"I have heard the other prisoners speak about you. The Vory. They say that you are a terrifying beast. That they have seen you rip the flesh from a man."

Valery looked up from under his brows. "Does that frighten you?"

"Sometimes we must become something we are not in order to survive."

"I'm an animal," he said, staring at nothing in particular.

"No, you are human." Father Ivanov let out a sigh. "You do not need to confess your sins to me, God already knows."

Valery picked at the dirt under the edge of his fingernail. "Is that why God continues to punish me?"

"God does not need to punish us, we punish ourselves much more without him. That is why we must also learn to forgive ourselves, Valery. It does not matter who you were, only who you decide to become."

"I'm glad you're doing better, Father." Valery stood and crossed the room, pounding on the door to signal the guard to let him out.

In time the snow melted and the sun began to warm the air again. Birds chirped in the distance along the treeline. The sun caressed Valery's face as he shoved his hands into the bowl of water before him, washing the stain of blood off his fingers. He ignored the moans coming from behind him as the prison guards dragged the tortured body of a man out.

"The Commander wants to see you," another guard said, poking his head through the doorway, his eyes scanning the mess on the floor. Valery removed the butcher's apron and grabbed his jacket off the hook on the wall, following the man out of the room.

The Commander paced across his office from the stove to the window, pausing long enough to greet Valery. "Sit down." The door closed, leaving the two men alone. He settled into his chair and leaned across his desk, his voice hushed. "It has not been formally announced yet, but Stalin is dead."

A lump formed in Valery's throat. With Stalin dead, all the rules were about to change.

"Beria will no doubt take over leadership, but no one knows what his next move will be for the Gulag. He never agreed with Stalin's tactics and paranoid retaliations. Some suspect that we may all face charges for carrying out his orders." He grabbed the bottle of vodka from the corner of his desk and pulled two glasses out from a drawer. Pouring two shots, he slid one across the desk for Valery.

Valery leaned forward and plucked the glass, tipping it back to let the cool liquid run down his throat.

"I wanted you to know that…" the Commander paused, as if the words were stuck in his throat. "I have arranged to have the priests released, I wanted you to know this."

"Thank you." Valery placed the glass back on the desk.

"Mikhail did you a favour having you sent here for his dirty work. If you were in Moscow right now there is no telling what the police might do to you. You have done your service for this country, as I have." He poured two more shots, quickly swinging his into his mouth and pouring another. "We will announce Stalin's death to the camp tonight after dinner. I have arranged to have you released during that time. It is my gift to you. If you are smart, you will disappear, Valya. Go live your life."

The Kazakh's words echoed in Valery's mind as he walked back to his cell. In a few hours he would be walking out of this prison. It had become his home. There was order, he knew what was expected of him. He knew his role. But outside those walls was an unpredictable world.

It wasn't safe to return to Moscow, not yet. Misha could wait.

Part Four

A Good Man

Chapter Thirteen

His small bag held bread and sausage. A hunting knife was shoved into the waste of his pants. Several guards shook Valery's hand as he walked out of the White Swan. He paused at the main gate at the end of the road, tempted for one final glance back, but instead inhaled long and slow before continuing on.

Dirt crunched under his boots as he continued to follow the road under the light of the moon. Solikamsk was quiet, smoke rising from the stacks of houses on the outskirts of town. He spent the night huddled under the warm vent at a factory with vacant thoughts. For the first time since he was a boy, he was alone. He had no home. No one to report to. No one to take care of him. No family. And no loyalty to anyone.

In the morning he continued north. There was nothing north but vast untouched land full of trees, wild animals, and a few scant villages which provided farming and logging services. He followed the Kama River until it met the Visher River. On the riverbank sat a small wooden fishing boat, the wood so weathered he almost wasn't sure it would still float. The oar was cracked, but could still steer in the water. For the next couple days he continued north, drifting along the river's meandering path.

When his food ran out he was forced to go to shore and hunt, but with only a knife he wasn't sure how he would do that. He'd never had to hunt before, no one had ever taught him. As a boy he stole food or ate what Misha provided. In prison, he always had something for his belly. In Moscow, he was able to purchase food in the market, and Katya would cook in his kitchen.

How did people survive alone in the wild?

A short ways up from the river he emerged into a clearing. A small barn and a quaint house sat nearby. A puff of smoke rose from the chimney, carrying with it the scent of meat. He crept to the nearest window to peek inside. A pot sat over the fire, a two large dogs lying on the floor in front of it. A shadow drifted past the window, Valery ducked his head. Slowly he brought his eyes to the ledge and peered back inside.

A young woman with long pale hair in a braid which hung off her shoulder busied herself, carefully cutting up a carrot at the table. As he glanced back towards the fire both the dogs slowly began to raise their heads and cast their eyes in his direction. He crept the short distance to the barn, quietly unlatching the door and slipping inside.

He pulled his lighter from his pocket and gave it a flick. The small warm flame wavered happily. Valery held it up to get a look at the surroundings. Two glowing eyes stared back at him from the horse standing lazily in its stall. It snorted in protest at him being there. He grabbed the small lantern hanging on a hook next to the stall and lit it. Suddenly the interior of the barn came to life revealing a horse cart and some farming tools.

Holding the lamp higher he spotted a hay loft to the right. The wooden ladder was frail and shook as he climbed. He nestled himself into the bales of hay and turned down the lamp, extinguishing the light. Once he was well rested he would figure out how to get some food.

Barking woke him. He curled himself into a tighter ball trying to warm up. Scant morning light seeped through the cracks in the walls reminding him he was no longer in prison.

"Okay, calm down you two." It was a female voice, cheerful, soft and melodic. Her footsteps stopped outside the barn and her laughter grew quiet. "Hello?" she called. "Is there somebody inside?"

He could hear the barn door creak and groan as she slowly pulled it open. The dogs burst through and continued their barking fits as they scurried about inside shoving their noses about and lifting them into the air. Valery glanced over the edge of the loft and found both dogs looking up at him, as soon as they spotted him they started barking again.

The woman slowly entered, a shotgun held firmly in her hands. "Hello? I have a gun."

The horse let out a snort, alerting the woman to its presence. Her hand reached out, waving in the air like a child until finally landing on the horse's nose. Her demeanor began to relax. "It's okay, Arina."

He watched as her hands slid along the wall until they found what they were looking for. Pulling the harness from where it hung on the wall, she carefully sliding it over the horse's head. After attaching a lead, she opened the horse's stall and began to lead it out of the bar. A few moments later the dogs followed suit, now tired of waiting for him to move.

Valery crawled over to one of the larger cracks in the wall and peered through, spying the young woman guiding the horse along the fenced pasture. She located the gate, pulled it open and took the horse inside. She removed the lead, but left the harness on, and then stepped out of the pasture so the horse could graze.

The dogs kept close to her, every once in a while brushed up against her legs, she bent down and gave them a rub. He could see her lips moving but was unable to hear what she was saying. Grabbing the scruff of fur on the back of the larger dog they made their way across the yard to the house.

Valery laid back in the hay and let out the breath he didn't realize he had been holding. It was time to move on. As he climbed down from the loft the rumble of a vehicle engine approached. Peaking between the crack in the open door he watched as a grey car scampered down the driveway and eventually came to a stop outside the house. Two men stepped out of the car, slamming the doors shut behind them. The dogs began to bark madly inside the house, but the young woman slipped through the front door, leaving them to their madness inside.

The men approached and began talking, but Valery was too far away to hear what they said. The woman appeared nervous and frightened of them as she clung to the door, her eyes never looking at them. A few more words were exchanged and finally he heard the woman say "No!", as the men glanced towards the horse in the pasture. The man nearest to her reached up and grabbed her by the hair, jerking her body into his as his other hand began to slide up her hip over her dress. She screamed, trying to resist him, but he laughed as he continued to taunt her.

Valery could feel a warmth building up inside him, he pulled his gloves off and dropped them on the ground next to his jacket. Pushing up his sleeves, he stepped out from the barn and headed towards the house, his hands clenched into fists at his sides.

"Is there something I can help you with, Comrades?"

The men's heads jerked around. Valery watched as with each step closer their eyes focused on the exposed tattoos on his arms and hands. The confidence on their faces began to fade when at last they spotted the edges of the tattooed knife and blood at Valery's neck.

The man holding the woman relaxed his grip, but refused to let her go. "No harm meant, Comrade, we were just playing."

Valery moved his eyes to the look of terror on the woman's face, tears streaming down her cheeks. "Are these men bothering you, devushka?"

Her body trembled as she nodded. "Yes." The word was barely audible from where he stood in front of the men's car.

"I think it's time you left."

"She owes us money," the second man spat out.

"Does she?" Valery said as he pulled his knife from the waist of his pants.

The man holding the woman released her and raised his hands out to the side. "We don't want any trouble. We had no idea that ..."

The two men stumbled as they made their way back to their car. "We'll expect the rest of it next month then, or we're taking the horse," the braver of the two men said as they got into the car. The engine roared to life, the wheels kicking up dirt and rocks as it sped from the yard.

The woman stood still, holding tightly onto the door frame, afraid to make a move. Valery took a couple steps closer to her, sheathing his knife in its case behind his back. He pulled the sleeves down on his thin sweater. "Are you all right?"

The woman slowly pulled her head away from the door frame and nodded. "Thank you." They both remained frozen where they were, each unsure what to do next.

Finally Valery decided that he should return to the barn and gather his things. He paused a moment, turning back to the woman. "I didn't mean to frighten you. I slept in your barn last night, I had nowhere else to say. I'll be on my way."

As he turned away she straightened herself. "Would you like some breakfast before you go?"

He stopped walking and turned back to her. "I don't wish to disturb you."

"Not at all. Please, come inside, it's the least I can do to thank you."

He inhaled long and deep, glancing about the yard before turning his attention back to her. "Thank you, my name is Valery."

"Svetlana," she replied as she began to open the door. Valery stopped in the doorway as he entered the small house, the dogs stood next to Svetlana and growled. "Don't worry about these two, they act much worse than they really are. Sit down," she said, motioning towards the table. She grabbed the hair on the back of one of the dogs as he had seen her do earlier, and they walked over to the stove.

Both dogs were Caucasian Ovcharkas, large mountain dogs, each weighed over a hundred pounds. Their fir was thick, mostly black and brown and appeared fluffy and dumb. The same dogs were used in the prisons, they could take down a large man easily and were far more intelligent than many gave them credit for.

Valery took a seat at the table, watching her ladle soup into a bowl. She turned back to him and took three careful steps towards the table, gently placing it down. She pulled a spoon from the pocket in her apron and placed it next to the bowl. "Eat, please."

Carefully he slid the bowl towards himself, watching as she turned back to the stove and poured herself a bowl, placing it down on the table where she had the first one. Valery watched her intently as she pulled out a chair and sat down. Her gaze remained transfixed in front of her, never one shifting to him. Was she avoiding him? Perhaps afraid of who he was? Everyone knew the Vory by their tattoos.

But after a couple minutes he pieced together the truth. "You're blind," he finally said.

She released her spoon and her hands dropped to her lap, her chin tipping down making it appear as if she were staring at the table. She nodded. "I was born this way."

She was still quite young, perhaps in her twenties. Very beautiful, Valery thought. "You do not have a husband?"

She shook her head. "I have always lived here with my parents." Her voiced dropped, "They're dead now."

"Why do you owe those men money?"

"They say my father owed them some money, they've been coming every month to collect on it."

"How much?"

"I'm not sure. They've already taken the cow and two other horses. If I lose Arina I'll be stuck here and have no way to get to the village."

"The horse?"

"Yes."

He took a spoonful of soup in his mouth, savouring the delightful flavors, it had been so long since he had tasted anything so delicious. Probably since Katya had last cooked for him.

"What kind of work do you do?" she asked, taking back up her spoon.

Valery pondered what to tell her. "I...I used to work for a prison."

A tentative smile spread across Svetlana's mouth. "That must have been why they seem so scared of you."

Valery couldn't help but chuckle, "Yes, that must have been it."

"What are you doing so far north?" she asked, dipping her spoon into her bowl.

"Stalin is dead," Valery replied, taking a bite of the chunk of meat on his spoon.

Svetlana froze, holding the steaming spoon on its way to her mouth. "He's...dead?"

Valery nodded, but then realized that she couldn't see him. "Yes, a few days ago."

She lowered her spoon back to her bowl. "What happened?"

"I'm not sure," Valery replied, intrigued by the concern on her face.

"He was such a great man," she breathed, her eyes beginning to tear up.

Valery opened his mouth to refute her claim, but closed it, realizing that she would never understand. "Yes," he finally said before shoving more soup in his mouth.

They sat in silence and continued to eat their soup, the dogs laying at Svetlana's feet. Valery's spoon jingled in his empty bowel as he pushed it forward. "Thank you, that was delicious."

Svetlana's lips turned up in a smile, but then quickly faded. "Where are you going? There's not much work up here. Some logging maybe."

Valery stared at her. "I'm not sure. Logging seems all right."

"My papa used to do some logging, he always said it was grueling work and not much fun."

"Do you have any other suggestions?"

"I hear there are factories being built. I'm not sure where, near Moscow I think."

"Anything closer to here?"

Svetlana placed her spoon in her bowl and clutched her hands in her lap. "You are welcome to stay here for a while. Spring is here and I will need some help planting in the garden. I'm sure the barn needs work. I can't pay you, but you are welcome to stay in the empty room and I will cook for you."

Valery's eyes darted around the house, noticing the scarce furnishings. He could see two bedrooms in the rear. The barn did need some work. And it would be quite difficult for her to till the soil by herself.

"All right, at least until I am able to find some other work, and then I'll be on my way."

Svetlana's face beamed as she tried to hide her joy.

"What would you like me to do?"

"Can you fetch some water? There are two bucket by the door, the pump in around back of the barn."

Valery left the house and returned to the barn to fetch his coat and gloves before wandering around back to find the water pump. As the buckets filled with water he couldn't help but take a moment to examine his surroundings. A cool breeze caressed his face. Birds chirped cheerfully in the nearby trees. The sun was beginning to cast its warmth through the parting clouds.

Was this what life was like for most people? No, this was a farm. This wasn't the city, or a village, or even a prison. But perhaps it was in some way how normal people lived. Her parents must have been normal.

On his way back to the house he could see Svetlana at the rear of the house trying to gather some wood in a small wheelbarrow. He watched as she maneuvered her way around the yard, not stopping until she heard the cart of the wheelbarrow knock against the side of the house.

Valery stepped up behind her and she nearly jumped at the sound of his voice. "Where would you like the buckets?"

Her hand flew to her chest, covering her heart as she gasped. "I didn't hear you, you move so quietly. Inside next to the stove."

Valery stepped past her, stopping in the doorway. "Leave the wood, I'll get it."

"Oh, it's not a problem. I can do it."

"No, I want to do it," he said.

Svetlana smacked her hands together as she tried to wipe off the dirt from the wood. "Thank you." She reached up, placing her hand on his back and followed him inside. She could feel his thick muscles moving through the coat, straining against the weight of the water. He was strong and broad. Tall. He moved with ease, even under the added strain.

Valery placed the buckets next to the wood stove, when he turned around he nearly bumped into Svetlana. He couldn't help but notice how the sun played with the golden strands of her hair. He was reminded how he used to watch the sun kiss Katya's brown hair giving it a golden sheen. Time seemed to slow as they stood there, Svetlana waiting patiently for him to move.

"Where would you like the wood?" he finally asked.

"A few pieces in the stove and the rest next to the fireplace for this evening."

He brushed past her and headed back out to retrieve the wood.

A short time later he found himself in the barn feeling the need to be alone. Sitting on a wooden crate he rested his elbows on his knees, his chin in his hands as she sat and listened to the silence around him.

The dogs came sniffing around the barn, alerting him that Svetlana was outside. The braver of the two approached him, sniffing at his arms and legs. He reached out, allowing his hand to stroke the dog's thick coarse hair. It turned, rubbing its head against him before darting off back outside.

Maybe being a farmer wouldn't be so bad. At least, for a little while.

Valery spent the next week getting the soil in the garden ready for planting. It was grueling work, but there was something about it that he enjoyed. Being outdoors with the sun beating down on his face. Moving his body. And at the end of the day he would wash himself in the barn, dress in some clothes which Svetlana had given him that once belonged to her father, and then return to the house for dinner.

It didn't take long for the two of them to establish a routine of work. Taking the time to sit and enjoy their meals together with some small talk and then continue on with their day. In the evening they would sit in front of the fire with the dogs. Valery found himself enjoying this time of day more and more. Svetlana would tell stories from her childhood, about her parents, and even about the dogs.

They sounded like fairy tales to Valery.

"What about you?" Svetlana asked one night. "Where did you grow up?"

Valery pulled his eyes from the fire and directed them at Svetlana. He inhaled long and slow contemplating what he could tell her. "For a short time as a boy I lived in Lipetsk."

"What did your parents do?"

"I was still very young, my mother stayed home with me. My father was in the military."

"Are they still alive?"

No, they're both dead." The two of them sat in silence for a few more moments before Valery stood. "I am going to bed. I'll see you in the morning."

Svetlana nodded, feeling the cool air brush past her hand as he walked past. "Valery?"

He stopped outside his door.

"I'm glad you're here."

"Good night, Sveta."

Chapter Fourteen

One morning Valery woke early, grabbed the rifle which used to belong to Svetlana's father, and headed into the woods. Nestling himself into the bushes at the edge of a glade he waited. Hunting a large animal wasn't much different than hunting a human. Just sit, and wait.

The sun began to peer over the treetops and cast its rays across the glade. A small doe stepped out from behind the trees and into the glade. It wasn't too big, but big enough to feed him and Svetlana for some time. And once he got good at hunting wild animals, they could sell some of the meat in the village and use the money to fix up the farm. Perhaps get a cow and some chickens, maybe a second horse.

Valery slowly brought the rifle up to his eye and took aim. He exhaled long and slow, then carefully pulled the trigger. The rifle knocked back into his shoulder, the shot echoing through the trees. He lowered the rifle and scanned the glade, tall grasses blocking his view. He hopped to his feet and ran across the glade.

A short distance from where he had seen the doe, she lay in the grass. A direct hit in the neck, her eye stared up at him full and round. Her chest still heaving in shock. He knelt next to her head, gently rubbing his hand down her snout, soothing her, before finally covering her eyes. With is other hand he pulled his knife free, positioned the tip at the base of the deer's neck between the front legs, and then quickly slid it in. The doe gave a sudden jolt and then stilled.

Hefting the deer over his shoulders Valery headed back to the farm. As he emerged from the edge of the field, a familiar car was parked next to the house. His heartbeat quickened. Just as he was about to drop the deer and run, a shot rang out, something piercing his right side. The jolt rocked through is body and his knees weakened. He crumpled to the ground, the deer thudding next to his head.

Wincing against the pain, Valery grabbed the rifle and brought the scope up to his eye. It took only a moment before he found the man ducked down next to the car. Steadying himself, he waited patiently for the man to appear again. And he would, he would want to check to make sure he hit his target. It didn't take long for the man to stand, staring across the field in Valery's direction. When he stepped out from behind the car Valery calmed his breathing, and squeezed the trigger.

The man's body whipped around, then fell to the ground. The front door of the house whipped open to reveal Svetlana clutched in the second man's grip, a handgun dug into her ribs. Using his elbows, Valery crawled through the tall grasses towards the house, setting himself up for another shot. The man holding Svetlana shouted for his comrade, but was met with silence. They inched their way further out of the house next to the car, coming to a halt when he finally found his dead friend.

"Show yourself, or I'll kill her!" he shouted into the silence.

Squeezing his hand against his ribs, Valery made his way around the barn, coming up on the side facing the house. The man continued to stare off towards the field, missing Valery as he made his way to the rear of the house. He paused just long enough to catch his breath, glancing down at the dark stain on his hand before forcing himself back to his feet.

He continued around the house, coming up on the opposite side, bringing him behind Svetlana and the man. Quietly he stepped forward until the tip of the gun barrel pressed into the man's back.

Immediately the man froze. "Well, you're a clever one, aren't you?"

"Svetlana, step away from the man," Valery's order was slow and commanding.

Small whimpers escaped her lips, but the man released his hold and she stepped away.

"Now come towards me," he said, encouraging her in his direction. "Slowly now, come towards my voice.

She did as he said, reaching her hand out to find him, but first making contact with the rifle. She flinched, a gasp caught in her throat.

"That's right, keep coming this way."

Tentatively she reached out again until she found his arm. Sliding down the length of it she continued until she met his shoulder.

"The house is to the left, go inside."

She nodded. Tears streamed down her cheeks along with a fresh bruise near her eye. Her hand shook as she waved her arms out in front of her trying to find her way forward.

As soon as he heard the door close, his finger pulled the trigger.

The man's body lurched forward, landing with a thud on the ground. Valery relaxed his grip on the rifle and dropped down, resting his arm across a raised knee to catch his breath.

He crawled his way to the house, his hand grasping at the door handle before it finally swung open. Svetlana sat crouched behind a chair, the dogs barking and scratching frantically from behind her bedroom door. "Sveta." He winced against the pain in his ribs. "I will need a needle and thread, can you find that for me?"

She nodded and crawled to the living room. Her hands dug through a basket and emerged with a small sewing kit clutched in her fingers.

Valery propped himself up against the wall and began to peel off his jacket. He glanced down at the dark liquid which was oozing from beneath his shirt. Carefully he peeled the fabric away to expose the wound.

"Valery? Where are you?" Svetlana asked, panic in her voice.

"I'm here, beside the door. Bring me what you have, then fetch me some fresh water and a cloth," he groaned from deep in his throat.

She took a few tentative steps towards the open door, then knelt and began to search with her hands to locate him. Once locating his leg, she followed it up his body, as she got to his hip her fingers became wet. "Have you been shot?"

A groan rumbled in his throat as he used the tip of his knife to dig the bullet out of his rib. "Now, Sveta. Hurry."

She dropped the sewing kit and quickly hurried into the kitchen to fetch some water and a clean cloth before returning to him. Valery groaned one last time before finally dislodging the bullet, it sprung from the wound, ticking across the wood floor until landing on a rug.

"Get the vodka from the cupboard," he ordered. Valery peeled his shirt off, sitting slouched against the wall. His exposed wound continued oozing dark liquid down his torso and onto the floor. He took the bottle of vodka from her, swallowed a large gulp before splashing some of the liquid against his wound. He growled against a clenched jaw, pressing his hand against the oozing hole to try and stop the bleeding.

Svetlana reached out, found the sewing kit, and pulled out a threaded needle. Valery instructed her to cup her hands with the needle and thread as he poured vodka over them.

"You're going to have to sew it up," he ordered as he reached out for her trembling hands and guided them towards the open wound. "It's small, just a couple stitches is all."

He slid his torso down onto the floor, trying to relax. Svetlana's fingertips rested gently against his warm skin. Her brows furrowed as she felt around the open wound, childhood scars and ink embedded in his skin bumped under her fingertips. Finally her fingers traced the edge of the small wound. She held the needle steadily between her fingers, pinched the skin, and then finally began to poke the needle through.

Valery's body flinched, his hand reaching out and grabbing hold of Svetlana's foot under the edge of her bum. He steadied his breathing and began to relax as she added a few more stitches. Finally, she cut the thread. Then dipping the clean cloth in the water she began to wipe it over Valery's body to clean the blood away. With each swipe she dragged her fingers across his skin as if trying to read the bumps.

Valery opened his eyes, gazing up at her, watching the concentration on her face before finally looking down at her hands tracing the outline of the two-headed swan next to the wound.

"You have many scars," she finally said.

Her touch was soothing. "Yes."

"Some are like pictures." He watched her hands move across his chest and outline the domes of the cathedral on his chest.

"They are tattoos."

"Tattoos?"

"Like pictures on the skin."

"What is this one?" she asked as she traced the swan again with her fingers.

"It's a two-headed swan."

"Why does it have two heads?"

"So that it can watch its back," he told her. It was a lie of course, but also a reminder for the future.

"You have so many."

"Yes."

Her hands began to slide further up his chest; he reached out, gently grasping them. "I need something to wrap my wound, do you have anything I can use for a bandage?"

Once he was finally bandaged, Valery pulled on a clean shirt and jacket and headed back outside to dispose of the bodies. Neither he nor Svetlana were going to be able to dig proper graves, and it was best not to attract the nose of a bear. Finally, he settled on burning them in the field and parking the car behind the barn to keep it out of sight until they could decide what to do with it.

Using the wheelbarrow he hauled the deer carcass into the barn, Arina eyed him suspiciously as he tied rope around it and pulled it up towards the rafters, allowing it hang freely. Svetlana had said that her father used to do that to drain the blood from a carcass, which was required before it could be cut up.

After he was done, Valery glanced down at the small dark stain on his shirt where the wound had leaked blood. He gently pressed his hand against it and inhaled. Arina snorted.

"I know," he said to the horse. "I was careless."

As he entered the house Svetlana turned around in the kitchen to face him. "I have some duck stew cooking, it should be done soon."

The dogs poked their noses up from where they lay on the floor near her.

Valery grunted his feet thudding across the floor as he went to his bedroom, ignoring her. He sat down on the bed hunched over, trying to relieve some of the pain from his ribs. Moments later Svetlana appeared in the doorway. "I found some more material you can use for fresh bandages. I can change it if you like?"

"I'll do it."

She reached forward handing him the bundle. "Thank you."

He winced as he looked up at her. "For what?"

"For being here. For everything that you've done. You are a good man, Valery." She walked away, leaving him with his own self-doubts.

He ate quickly and then went to bed, Sveta's words still echoing in his mind, *"You are a good man, Valery."* Was he a good man? Did good men torture and kill prisoners? Did good men kill Vory bosses?

His body jerked awake in the middle of the night. As he lay still he could hear faint breathing beside him. The moonlight coming through the window cast a glow across Svetlana's face where she lay peacefully. Without thinking, he reached up and pulled a lock of hair away from her face, she nuzzled herself closer, pressing into his shoulder. Gently he pulled the blanket she had wrapped around her up over her exposed shoulder. One of the dogs snorted where it slept on the floor beside them.

Chapter Fifteen

Valery rose early the next morning, sliding carefully out of bed so as not to disturb Svetlana. He lit a fire in the kitchen stove and put on a pot of water. Once boiled, he prepared a pot of tea. As the tea steeped, he ventured out to the barn and moved Arina to the pasture before heading back into the house.

Pouring tea into a cup, he could hear the clicking of the dog toenails against the floor indicating that Svetlana was probably awake. Soft footfalls padded against wood out of his bedroom and Svetlana emerged, her hair slightly disheveled, her hands clenching the blanket wrapped around her.

"Valery?"

"I'm in the kitchen." Her shoulders relaxed as she came towards him.

"I'm sorry...I."

"It's fine," he replied. Even he didn't want to admit that it was nice having her lying next to him all night.

Valery leaned against the counter watching her begin to move about the kitchen. It dawned on him that what happened yesterday must have been terrifying for her. When she reached towards the cupboard Valery turned quickly and snatched a cup for her, their arms brushing. "Here," he said, gently placing it in her hand.

He watched her pour some tea and take a sip of the hot liquid.

Valery inhaled long and slow before finally opening his mouth. "How are you, Sveta?"

She lowered the cup down to the counter, her brows coming together creating small wrinkles on her forehead. A tear slid down her cheek as her chin tilted down.

He turned, bringing her into his arms in an enveloping hug. Her body melted against him as she sniffled. "Everything will be okay, you're safe. I'm not going anywhere."

"What if someone comes looking for them?"

It was a possibility. "Then we just tell them that we haven't seen them." He would have to get rid of the car.

After a long minute she finally said, "I heard once in the village that men with tattoos belong to the Vory v Zakone."

"Most of them do, yes."

"Do you?" Her voice was soft and quiet.

He relaxed his hold of her, waiting for the moment when she would pull away from him. "I did…once."

Her hands gripped his shirt, holding him tighter.

He held her close, enjoying this moment between them. It had been a long time since he had a woman in his arms. Since Katya.

"I'm going to go move the car somewhere and hide it in the woods. I'll be back this afternoon." Svetlana nodded as their bodies began to separate, her hands still clenching his shirt, afraid to let go of him. Valery leaned forward and placed a gentle kiss on her forehead. "I'll be back in time for lunch. And I'll be hungry, Sveta. Make something good," he chuckled as he grabbed his coat off the back of a chair and headed out of the house.

The car roared to life. Although cars were quite common in Moscow, they weren't as common in the countryside. The car was a ZIS 110, the Zavod imeni Stalina. Named after Stalin himself. Whoever those men were, they were connected to power. They weren't Vory, which meant most likely they were connected to politics, perhaps a regional commissar.

But people disappeared all the time in Russia.

Valery drove for nearly an hour, the sun had now climbed above the treeline. He found a dirt road which disappeared into some trees. Turning onto it, he drove further, finally parking the car in the brush. He glanced back only once at it as he considered driving all the way to Moscow, but not yet. He was a good man now, and he enjoyed this life he had created on the farm with Svetlana. It wasn't time to return to Moscow.

The walk back to the farm was long, but Valery found himself in a hurry to return. The sun beat down, reminding him of his freedom and his new life. Gone were the days of always watching his back. Gone were the long exhausting hours spent in small rooms inflicting pain on people. For the first time in his life, Valery was looking forward to a future.

As he turned down the small road to the farm he could see Svetlana hanging laundry out on the line next to the house. The dogs lazily laid in the sun nearby. The crunch of the dirt beneath his boots alerted her of his approach. She lowered her arms and turned in his direction. "Valery?"

"I thought I told you I would be hungry."

A smile beamed from her face and she laughed. "There is some stew on the stove, it should be almost done."

He towered over her. Reaching up he tucked some stray hairs behind her ear, his thumb gently rubbing the soft skin. Her hands raised to his face, and for the first time he allowed her to touch him. Small delicate fingers slid over his features as if tracing a picture of him in her mind, heavy brows, a strong nose, wide lips, and chiselled jaw.

When her fingers returned to his mouth he smiled, her face lighting up with his.

"You are much more handsome than I thought," she said.

A chuckle rumbled in his chest. "And you are far more beautiful than you know, Krasotka."

The months seemed to drift by in a hazy dream. Every day Valery was sure he would wake up and be back in prison, but every day he would roll over and Svetlana would still be lying next to him.

It was a warm morning, the sky was clear and the sun beat down. Valery stood in the barn staring up at the large deer carcass, admiring how good he was getting at removing the organs from the body, which now lay in a heap on the ground, the dogs lapping up their favourite parts. Gripping his knife, his hands and arms still covered in blood, he stepped out of the barn and into the sun. Temporarily blinded, he raised his arm up to shield his view. The sun felt good on his bare chest.

He began to walk towards the bucket of water he had left out to wash the blood off with. In the distance, two small figures approached the farm on the road, riding in a small horse drawn cart similar to the one Svetlana kept in the barn. There was a scream and the cart came to a stop. Valery could see the man who had been leading the horse drop the reins and pull up a gun, pointing it directly at him.

"Svetlana!" he shouted, panic in his voice. "Svetlana!" He jumped down from the cart and slowly approached Valery.

Valery stood still, his arms hanging relaxed at his sides as he watched the man approach him.

"Where is Svetlana?" He glanced around, nervously approaching Valery. "Svetlana!" Suddenly the man froze, his eyes going wide as he noticed not only the blood on Valery's body, but the array of tattoos. He gripped the gun tighter. "What have you done with her?"

Valery opened his mouth to answer, but wasn't sure what good it would do.

Finally the front door of the house opened and Svetlana emerged, the sun causing her golden hair to glow. Her face beamed. "Andrei? Is that you?"

"Sveta, who is this man? Are you all right?"

Using a stick, she began to walk forward towards his voice, the stick tapping along the ground. "Valery?"

"I'm here," he replied, reassuring her. "But your friend has a gun pointed at me."

"No! Andrei, lower your gun."

"Who is this man?" Andrei shifted the butt of the gun into shoulder, refusing to lower it. "Why is he here?"

"Valery has been staying with me, he helps around the farm."

"He is from prison, Sveta. He's a Vor," he said, his voice growling out the words in distaste.

"I know," she replied as she came up to him. "Lower your gun, Andrei. Valery has never harmed me, in fact, he saved my life."

Andrei eyed Valery suspiciously, his eyes still focused on his body. "Why are you covered in blood?"

"I just gutted a deer in the barn, go look if you like."

Andrei huffed and lowered his gun.

"Did Olga come with you?" Svetlana asked.

"She's in the cart, I will go get her and be back." Andrei grunted as he set off back to his wife.

"I frightened him," Valery said.

"Well, you don't frighten me," Sveta replied and smiled.

"Yes, well you can't see me right now."

"Andrei will be fine. He's old. He and Olga were friends with my parents."

Valery began to splash water on himself and wash the blood away as Andrei and Olga brought the horse and cart closer to the house. Olga's eyes bulged from her face in fear at the sight of Valery. He grabbed his shirt from the fence post and pulled it on before turning back to their guests.

Olga kissed Svetlana's cheeks as they greeted, whispering something in her ear Valery was unable to hear. Svetlana's brows furrowed and she shook her head. "I'm fine, Olga. Valery is a good man."

Valery followed everyone into the house and they gathered around the small kitchen table. He took the kettle from Svetlana's hands to put the water on the stove for tea, then pulled a chair out for her to sit.

Andrei refused to take his eyes off Valery, suspicion in his glare.

"So what brought you here?" Svetlana asked to break the silence. "You haven't been since Christmas."

Olga reached forward and gently grabbed Svetlana's hand. "We would have come sooner but we were both quite ill for a while." She paused as she looked at her husband, and then briefly to Valery. "We brought some dried fish and extra potatoes."

"Oh, thank you. My garden didn't produce much last year. Valery has been helping out, and this year we're hoping there will be a lot more. In fact, Valery was even able to plant some corn in the far field. We're hoping maybe eventually we can expand the crop if it does well, and then we can sell it in the market." Svetlana's face beamed with pride.

Valery rose from his seat and attended to the tea, bringing the pot and cups to the table for everyone.

"How did you end up here?" Andrei asked as Valery returned to his chair.

Valery clasped his hands on the table and inhaled before looking up at Andrei. "I was released from prison the day Stalin died. I had nowhere else to go, so I came north. I found Sveta's farm along the way."

"Father's debt collectors were harassing me," Svetlana jumped in. "Valery was able to get them to leave." She slid her hand across the table towards Valery, and he reached over to gently clasp it. "He's been a great help."

Andrei shifted in his chair, still not satisfied with the answer. "Your tattoos, you have a high rank," he said, pointing to his shoulder as he looked at Valery's.

"I do." Valery sat calmly, watching Andrei's face. "You know a lot about the Vory."

"I spent five years in the Gulag. You look like you've spent quite a number of years there yourself." This time he tapped his finger on his chest.

"I have. Ever since I was a boy. I was first sent to the Gulag when I was twelve."

Svetlana gasped under her breath, Valery gave her hand a reassuring squeeze. "My parents were both dead and I was an orphan. A man in Siberia took me in."

"He was Vor?" Andrei asked.

"He was. It is the only life I've known, until I met Svetlana."

Noting the sincerity in Valery's voice, Andrei relaxed and began to pour his wife and himself some tea.

"Svetlana is lucky to have you," Olga chimed in.

As the women busied themselves in the garden under the afternoon sun, Valery showed Andrei around the farm where they discussed ideas on improvements. Andrei even offered some hunting advice, as they discussed techniques for preserving meats. And as they were preparing to leave Valery was sure to give them a hind quarter from the deer hanging in the barn.

"That went well," Svetlana said, as she began to cut a potato in the kitchen.

Valery stepped up behind her sliding his arms around her waist, resting his chin on her shoulder. "For a moment I almost thought he might actually shoot me."

Svetlana rubbed her hand along his arm. "I might not be able to see what they see on the outside, Valya, but I see who you are on the inside. And now they do too."

He sighed and gave her cheek a kiss. "I can never escape my past, Sveta. If you knew of the things I've done…"

She turned around and slid her arms around his waist in an embrace, pressing the side of her face against his chest to listen to his heartbeat. "You survived, that is all I need to know. And for that I am grateful."

Chapter Sixteen

When the fall began to blow its biting winds, and branches on the trees were becoming bare, Valery finally agreed to take Svetlana into town. In the cold weather he would be able to cover up his tattoos under layers of clothing, and wear gloves on his hands without arising suspicion. Arina pulled the cart, her hooves pounding against the ground proudly.

They made their way to the farmer's market. It didn't take long to sell the dried corn, meats, and baked goods they had brought. Valery tugged at the scarf around his neck, making sure that it covered his tattoo. He found himself watching the people conversing around them, bartering deals, telling jokes. Children played nearby chasing a cat.

It was all so normal, he assumed. Dull and predictable. Everyone was happy, smiles on their faces, laughter. This was how people lived. It reminded him of a good day in prison, everyone joking and laughing and getting along. His suddenly body tensed, on days like that something always eventually would spark a fight. Someone always died on those days.

Valery spent the day expecting the worst.

With the money they purchased some rope and building supplies to fix up the barn and the house. It was only early in the afternoon, but the sun was already beginning to set when they headed back to the farm. The sky was clear and the stars sparkled brightly in the night sky by the time they returned home. As Svetlana went in the house to prepare dinner, Valery unharnessed Arina and let her wander the pasture while he unloaded all their goods and returned the cart to the barn. The dogs ran about the farm in a game of chase, excited to be out of the house.

Frantic barking erupted from outside the barn, the type of barking which meant that the dogs had discovered an intruder. Valery grabbed the rifle next to the door and headed outside.

Svetlana poked her head out from the house. "What's going on?"

"Get back inside, I'll check it out," he called out to her as he slipped into the field behind the barn, following the dogs' frantic calls.

On the edge of the treeline Valery caught sight of a large shadow. He whistled for dogs, causing them to momentarily pause. After a second whistle and a shout they finally abandoned their guard and came running back to him. Quickly he locked them in the barn while he brought Arina back inside, once the horse was secure he took the dogs with him back to the house.

Svetlana raised her head from where she stood over the stove stirring a pot. "What was it?"

Valery leaned the rifle beside the door. "I'm not sure, it might have been a bear." He pressed a kiss against the top of her head. "I'll check tomorrow when there's more light and make sure it's gone."

By the next morning there was a fluffy layer of snow on the ground, making it impossible to locate any evidence of their visitor from the day before. Valery even went so far as the river, where he discovered the weathered remains of the small wooden boat he had used the year before. But there were no signs of the animal even in the freshly fallen snow. Whatever it had been, it was now long gone.

For the next few days Valery kept a close watch on the farm as heavier snows began to fall. After taking care of Arina in the mornings and making sure she was warm and fed in the barn, Valery and Svetlana spent their days indoors by the fire.

Svetlana's fingers worked nimbly as she knit. Valery watched her in awe, wondering how it was possible that she was able to do so much without ever seeing. "Do you ever wish that you could see?" he finally asked.

Svetlana's hands stopped moving. "I used to, when I was a kid. I've always wanted to see a sunset, or the snow falling. My mama used to try to describe things to me, but it was no use because I having nothing to relate it to. I don't even know what I look like."

"You look how the sun feels when it warms your face on a cold day."

Svetlana smiled, closing her eyes and imaging how that would feel. "That always makes me feel so good. It's as if an angel is caressing my cheek."

"That's how you feel to me, like an angel who rescued me from the cold."

A tear trickled down her cheek, she tried to wipe it away before Valery could see. He leaned over and wiped another away. "Why are you crying?"

"I always thought that you were my angel, Valya. You saved me. I don't know how I would have survived much longer if you hadn't come along when you did. I had been praying to God to help me, and he sent you."

Valery sat back, distancing himself from her. "I don't deserve you, Sveta."

She leaned into his side and he instinctively put his arm around her. "Yes you do."

They celebrated Christmas that year by roasting a rabbit over the fire. Valery threw a couple pieces of meat onto the floor and the dogs excitedly lapped them up, slurping and smacking their mouths. For the New Year they ventured down the road the short distance to celebrate with Andrei and Olga, feasting on a fat duck and sweet baked goods washed down with vodka.

"I hope you don't mind me asking," Andrei started, "but I'm curious. These," he pointed to his shoulders. "What rank is that?"

Valery leaned forward on the stool where he sat next to the fire, glancing at the women in the kitchen before returning his gaze to Andrei. "It is Avtoritet."

"That is a high rank?"

"It is."

"On your hands, I see you were an orphan and you have murdered, but I noticed you had VOHRA on one of your shoulders too. You worked for the NKVD."

"Yes." Valery took a sip of his vodka.

"Does that not make you a traitor to the Vory?"

"It does." Valery inhaled and exhaled long and slow. "It was the only way I thought I could get out."

"But this one," Andrei pointed to the ring tattoo of the crown and dagger. "This one I've never seen before. What does it mean?"

Valery spread out his fingers and looked down. "I killed a Pakhan."

Andrei's eyes grew wide and he lowered his voice even more so the women wouldn't hear him. "But…then that would make you…"

"No, it doesn't," Valery said. "I was told to do it. Ordered. That's how I ended up in prison again."

"You have a lived a very hard life. I am sorry for all you have been through." They sat in silence a moment before Andrei spoke again. "Sveta is right, you are a good man, Valery. You have been very good to her, and Olga and I are very grateful for that."

"She has been very good to me." As Valery glanced up he caught Svetlana smiling and laughing with Olga and for the first time felt a warmth rise up in his chest.

Several nights later Valery woke in the middle of the night, something was outside digging and scrapping next to the house. Svetlana was peacefully asleep beside him. He glanced down at the dogs who had their heads raised, ears twitching about trying to catch the sounds outside. He slid from the bed and went over to the window to try and see what it could be. A large shadow bobbed around the corner of the house and then disappeared.

Valery padded through the house ignoring the cold floor on his bare feet as he ran to the kitchen window, making it just in time to see the shadow bound across the yard towards the barn. There was just enough moonlight to see the large shadow rise up on its hind legs and begin to press itself again the barn door, causing Arina to spook inside and begin to call out.

Valery dashed back to the bedroom and began to pull on his clothes. Svetlana stirred sleepily in bed. "What's going on?"

"Stay here. I think there's a bear trying to get into the barn."

Valery launched himself out of the bedroom, the dogs following with a stirring excitement. Quickly he pulled on his jacket, boots, and gloves, then grabbed the rifle next to the door and checked it for bullets. As he threw open the door the dogs bound past him before he could stop them.

Valery raised the gun and took aim towards the shadow in front of the barn, hoping to spook it away before the dogs got close enough. The gun went off, the echo moving about the farm in every direction. The creature paused and turned towards him.

The dogs barked rabidly, stopping a short distance away from the animal which now stood staring at them. Valery raised the gun and fired another shot, this time spooking the animal enough that it took off across the field towards the treeline, the dogs in hot pursuit. Valery whistled after them and shouted, but they ignored him as they dove into the woods.

Valery's boots sunk deep into the snow nearly to his knees as he tried to make his way across the field after them. The barking began to grow distant and more frantic. A low groaning roar was followed by a squeal from one of the dogs, the other one still barking madly. There was a second roar followed by a second squeal from the other dog and everything fell silent. Valery stopped at the treeline and fired off another shot through the trees.

The echo disappeared quickly into the forest and everything fell silent. Valery squinted, hoping to see something in the darkness, but it was impossible. As quickly as he could, he made his way back to the barn and grabbed the lantern inside, lit it, and then returned to the treeline holding the flickering flame out in front of him.

Carefully he began to step forward into the dark abyss. The trees seemed to jump out at him, blocking his every move as he dipped and slid between them. Faint whimpering drew him forward until he finally located one of the dogs, its breathing heavy. A large gash had torn open a small part of its abdomen, dark liquid spread out on the snow around it.

Valery knelt at its side, his hand gently caressed the animal's head. Finally he stood up, raised the gun and took aim, putting the creature out of its misery. As everything went quiet again Valery listened closely for sounds of the second dog, finally locating it a short distance away where it had been throw up against a tree and now lay in a heap on the ground unable to move. One of its eyes bulged from its head.

The chest rose and fell faintly, but there was no way to save it. Again, Valery brought the gun up and took aim, only this time he hesitated. A wave of sadness swept over his face, warm tears begin to well in his eyes. Quickly he wiped them away and fired the gun.

Alone, Valery emerged from the woods, checked on Arina and secured the barn before heading back into the house.

Svetlana was now up, a fire going in the stove as she put a pot of water on. When the door closed she turned around, listening intently. "Did you get it? Where are the dogs?"

"No. The dogs are gone."

"They've run after it?"

"They did. It attacked them. They're dead."

Svetlana brought her hands to her mouth to stifle her small weep.

Valery set the rifle down and shrugged off his jacket. "I'm going back to bed." His feet thudded past Svetlana and into the bedroom, the door knocked shut behind him.

Part Five

The Beast

Chapter Seventeen

When Valery woke he was alone in bed. The house was quiet and still. Too still. He glanced at the rug on the floor where the dogs normally slept. When he emerged from the bedroom he found Svetlana snuggled up in a blanket on the floor next to the stove. He knelt down beside her and gently swept the hair from her face. Her eyes batted open, and for a brief moment it was as if she was actually looking at him.

"I'll ask Andrei if he knows someone who has dogs. We'll find two more." He slid his hand along the soft skin of her cheek and she nodded, bringing her hand up to his and holding him there.

A few days later Valery ventured into the village. He didn't like the idea of leaving Svetlana at home alone, but it would be quicker for him to go alone. He wandered the small market asking around about dogs. "Try back in a couple months," everyone told him.

Muffled sounds of music and chatter hummed through the walls of the unassuming building. Valery yanked open the door, his eyes scanned the pub as he stepped inside. In the far corner one face immediately caused him to halt in his tracks. Efim. What could he be doing there? It was too much of a coincidence. He sat with a second man in deep conversation, just as Valery turned to leave, Efim looked up and caught his eye. His face paled and his eyebrows rose. Valery paused long enough to give him a warning glare before walking out the door.

The snow crunched under his heavy feet as he marched down the street towards the market where he had left Arina at a stable. A door slammed closed behind him followed by hurried feet in the snow.

Valery stopped walking and turned to meet Efim, causing the skinny man to immediately come to a halt a short distance away. A sly, wide grin spread across his face.

"I never thought I'd be seeing you again," Efim chuckled under his breath. "Misha didn't think you'd ever make it out of the Swan again, but I knew you had your ways. I warned him you'd get out again, but we always thought you'd return to Moscow."

Valery remained stoic as he stood and watched. His hands clenched into fists.

"But then I got a message that an old man had been asking around about some very specific tattoos up here. Imagine my surprise. I thought, no, that couldn't be our Valya. Released from prison already?"

Valery took one step towards Efim, causing the man to suddenly stumble back a step.

"Naturally I had to come and see if the rumors were true. There he is, the Beast lives, emerged from hiding."

"If you value your life, you'll leave and never speak of this," Valery finally said.

"Oh don't worry, I'll leave. But I can't guarantee I won't be back, and I won't be alone. It's your turn to be hunted." Efim threw he head back and bellowed before turning on his feet, heading back to the pub.

Valery remained standing, refusing to move until Efim was out of sight. As soon as the pub door closed he whipped around and quickly headed back to the market. Retrieving Arina, he pushed the old horse as fast as she could run back to the farm. It was mid-afternoon, but the sun was already setting when he finally got Arina secured in the barn. He kicked the snow from his boots and entered the house.

Svetlana raised her head up from where she sat on the couch in front of the fire. "How did it go?"

"We'll have better luck in the spring when there are new pups."

"Yes, of course."

Valery glanced around the stark house which had been more like a home for him than he'd ever had in his life. His eyes rested on Svetlana with her knitting needles clicking in her hands. He stepped over to her, towering before her, his presence looming quietly.

Her hands stopped moving and she tilted her head to the side. "I can feel you standing there. What is it?"

Valery knelt before her and gently took her hands in his. "Have you ever thought about leaving here?"

Her brows wrinkled. "Where would I go?"

"Somewhere else. Further south perhaps, where it's warmer. Imagine the crops we could grow."

"And start over?"

"Of course."

"But this is my home, Valya. Our home."

He let out a sigh and rested his forehead against the soft skin of her hands. "It would be safer. I understand if you don't want to leave, but just think about it."

Svetlana slid one of her hands free and ran her fingers through his hair. "I've never been anywhere else. Do you think our family would be safer there?"

"It's very safe... What do you mean, our family?" Valery raised his head to look at Svetlana's face, a smile delicately turned up on her lips.

"We're going to have a baby, Valya."

Valery became still, never taking his eyes from Svetlana. She brought her hands to his face and traced his lips. "Are you not happy?"

He grabbed her hands and gently kissed her fingers. "I'm very happy. All the more reason to move if there is a bear around the farm."

"If you think it is best, then yes. But it will have to wait until spring. Do you think once we get there we would still have time to plan a garden?"

"Plenty of time, spring and summer run longer there."

As soon as the weather permitted they would load up their cart, hitch Arina, and then began the long trip south. There was no telling when Efim would return, and he would not return alone, but with a small army of Vory. If they knew about Svetlana it would only add fuel to their sadistic plans, raping and beating her over and over in front of him, before finally putting her out of her misery and then turning on him.

He would never let that happen.

Chapter Eighteen

A few days later Andrei rode up to the house, he slid off his horse and rushed across the yard towards Valery. Valery split one more piece of wood before swinging his ax into the stump and leaving it.

He raised his hand up to shield the sunlight from his eyes. "Andrei, it is nice to see you again." Valery recognized the panic across the man's face. "What is it?"

"I overheard some men in the village asking about you. I think they were Vory. Luckily, no one in the village knows about your tattoos." He rubbed his hand over his face and grew solemn. "I think I may have accidentally led them on that you were in the area. After our very first meeting I had asked around, some men who had been in the Gulag, if they knew what some of your tattoos meant. I'm sorry."

"It's okay. You may have let on that I was around. I ran into an old friend a few days ago in the village that is why they are searching for me. I'm hoping they'll just leave. If I was smart, I would have left that night." Valery looked back towards the house. "But I could never do that to Sveta."

"What will they do if they find you?"

Valery stared off into the distance. "Things which no man in his right mind would dare to think about."

Andrei grabbed his shoulder firmly. "You need to leave."

"Yes, I have convinced Sveta that we should go south, but she refuses to leave until the spring."

"You may not have a choice."

Valery crossed his arms over his broad chest, his eyes dropping to his feet. "She's pregnant."

Andrei cursed under his breath. "I wish I could say congratulations but... This farm is far enough away from the main roads, they may not find you."

"But they will never stop looking."

"Best to stay away from the village."

"I agree."

"I'll let you know if I hear more."

"Thank you. I've never had someone..."

Andrei reached out and squeezed Valery's arm. "Sveta is right, you are a good man, Valery. You have been very good to her. And you are like a son to me now, I will do what I can to help."

Andrei got back on his horse and thudded down the road, disappearing behind the trees towards his own farm. Svetlana emerged from the house, "Did I hear Andrei?"

Valery drop the cord of wood by the door. "It was."

"What did he want? I could have put tea on."

"He may know someone who might have some pups for us soon." Valery gave her cheek a quick kiss and stepped inside.

With each passing day Valery grew more tense, spring was nearly upon them but the snow refused to melt. Large flakes fell from grey clouds which seemed to light up the night sky. Valery stood watching from the kitchen window lost in his own thoughts.

"You have been standing there for a long time," Svetlana said from the couch.

Valery inhaled suddenly. "It's snowing again."

"It feels like winter will never end."

"Yes."

"Are you worried the bear will return?"

"We'll be fine." Valery glanced towards the road before finally pulling himself away from the window and sitting down next to Svetlana. The house grew silent, only the crackle from the fire entertaining them. Valery watched the flames dancing wildly as he slipped back into his thoughts.

He would need to go after Efim. He needed to end this before they found him. Svetlana and the baby would never be safe if he stayed.

"I need to go to Moscow," he finally said. "There is something I need to take care of."

Svetlana's hands went still. "How long will you be gone?" Her voice was quiet and trembled.

"Not long." He leaned forward, resting his elbows on his knees. "There are men in the village looking for me. If I stay, that will put you in danger. I will get Olga and Andrei to check in on you." He rose and then disappeared into the bedroom.

Valery's eyes burst open to the sound of knocking, he lay still a moment trying to remember where he was. Muffled voices drifted back from the front of the house. A scream from Svetlana caused him to sit up, his heart pounding heavy against his ribs.

The door slammed shut and heavy feet thudded across the floor followed by laughter and more muffled voices. Valery grabbed his knife and shoved it into the back of his pants as he stood. He crept to the edge of the doorway and peered towards the front of the house.

"We know he's been staying here, your old friend was very insistent even as we slit his throat."

Svetlana gasped, her hands pressing over her mouth. As Efim approached her Valery stepped from the room. "Stop."

Efim froze a moment before suddenly reaching out and grabbing Svetlana, pulling her body in front of his. "The Beast has risen," he sneered.

Valery glanced from Efim to the two other young men near the door. Their eyes grew wide and their bodies began to tremble as Valery eyed them up. The rifle still sat next to the door behind them. His eyes snaked their way back to Efim. "Let her go, she is not part of this."

"You've been playing house, Valya. You remember what happened last time."

"Leave her, she knowns nothing."

Efim brought his knife blade up to her throat, gently scraping it against her skin. Svetlana wept, tears streaming down her face. "Val," she whimpered.

"Leave her, and I will go with you."

Efim's eyes nearly bulged from his head, before his brows came down as he peered at Valery. "No, Comrade, we can't do that. She's see our faces."

"She's blind," Valery countered.

Efim cast a glance at Svetlana, studying her eyes before finally returning his glare to Valery. "That explains why she never ran screaming from you. One look at you and... Well it's probably a good thing, then she won't be able to see what we're about to do to you." Efim nodded towards his two comrades, "Get him."

The two young men hesitantly took steps forward, brandishing their own large knives in their hands. Valery stood his ground calmly, his stature impressive and intimidating against their lithe, weasely frames. They took a step forward, Valery countered with his own step forward, causing them to pause and glance at one another.

"Take him," Efim shouted, spurring the two young men into action.

They lunged forward swinging wildly. Valery countered one blade as he pulled his own from behind his back and shoved the knife between the man's ribs, pulling it out quickly as he spun around. The second man's blade just made contact with Valery's arm, slicing through his shirt and leaving a tiny thin line of blood.

Still holding onto his first victim, Valery threw him at the second man, knocking him back as the body fell to the floor with a thud. Somewhere behind him Svetlana's screams became muffled. The young man steadied himself and charged at Valery a second time. Valery ducked under his arm and rolled towards the front door, his hand reached out and snatched the rifle. As he rolled onto his shoulder he turned back, pointed the rifle and pulled the trigger.

An explosion thundered through the house.

The young man froze where he stood about to charge Valery. Suddenly his knees buckled and he collapsed to the floor. Valery immediately turned the gun towards Efim who stood shielding himself with Svetlana, one hand held firmly over her mouth, the other pressing his knife against her throat.

"Don't even think about it. I'll slice her throat before you can pull the trigger."

Svetlana whimpered, tears streaming down her face. Valery took in the scene as he gathered his thoughts. His eyes scanned every gesture as he looked for a weakness he could take advantage of. And then he found it, clutched in Svetlana's hand, pressed to her side, was a knitting needle.

"Sveta," he said, getting her attention. Her body calmed a moment as she focused on his voice. "When this is all over I will have to get you some new knitting needles." Her hand clenched the long thin needle in her hand. "Now!"

With a sudden jolt of energy at Valery's command, Svetlana twisted her body and rammed the knitting needle into Efim's chest. As Efim clutched at his chest and gasped, as Svetlana's hands clutched at her own throat, dark liquid beginning to seep between her fingers.

Efim fell to the floor and Valery dashed across the room and caught Svetlana, gently guiding her down until she was laying on her back. Her hands squeezed her neck but couldn't stop the flow of blood. Valery grabbed the small blanket from the couch and began to wrap it around her neck.

"You're fine, you'll be all right. I got you," he said, trying to calm her.

Efim laughed between garbled gasps as he coughed up blood. "I told you."

Svetlana opened her mouth to try to speak, blood burbling up. Valery held her tight, pressing his forehead against hers. "Shh, Krasotka. You'll be all right, I'm here." He pressed his lips against her cheek. "I'm sorry."

Slowly her eyelids closed and she fell limp in his arms.

Valery sat hunched over her lifeless body a moment, when he lifted his head his eyes landed on Efim under heavy brows.

Efim's complexion paled.

"You're gonna wish you were dead by the time I'm done with you," Valery growled out.

Chapter Nineteen

"It was Misha, he ordered it," Efim spat out, choking on the dark liquid bubbling from his mouth.

Valery rose to his feet, grabbed Efim by the collar and dragged him out of the house and through the snow. He kicked the barn door open, spooking Arina in her stall. The pale light outside was just enough for him to find the ropes he kept dangling from the rafters. He tied one to each of Efim's wrists and began to hoist him up.

"Do you know why they call me The Beast?"

Efim choked, spitting out blood as he watched Valery light a lamp and hang it next to the horse stall, Arina snorting at him.

He stopped in front of Efim and began to roll up his sleeves. "When I was still a boy I was sent to the White Swan. They threw me into a crowded cell with grown men. I was still skinny, prey for their hungry eyes. And in the middle of the night they held me down while the Vor Lieutenant raped me over, and over, and over."

Valery paused, inhaled long and slow and pulled his knife from the waist of his pants, holding it up before Efim's face. "I prayed that I would die that night, left naked and cold. Torn and bleeding on the floor where the guards found me the next morning. The prison Commander took pity on me. I don't know why."

Using the knife, Valery began to cut at Efim's shirt, tearing strips away as he spoke. "He asked me what justice I wanted against this man. So I told him. I told him that I wanted to make him pay for what he did to me."

Blood dripped from the knitting needle still shoved into Efim's chest, slowly trailing down his torso.

"So the Commander brought the man to the prison yard and tied him to a post and shoved a knife in my hand." Valery paused as he cut away Efim's pants, leaving him hanging bare in the cold night, goosebumps rising on his skin.

Valery glanced up, meeting Efim's eyes. "I think he thought I would just slit his throat and be done with it, if I could even do that. But do you know what I did?"

Efim nodded and Valery raised an eyebrow. "I'm not going to do that to you Efim. I could never do that to you." Efim let out a sigh. "What I'm going to do to you will be much worse, Efim, much worse." His body tensed as he watched Valery raise his hand and push the knitting needle further into his chest.

"It's Misha you should be mad at. This was all Misha," Efim pleaded and choked to deaf ears. "He was insulted when you turned on him. He'd been planning his revenge for years,"

Valery inserted the point of his knife into Efim's arm and dragged it down to his hand, watching the skin split open and dark liquid begin to drip from the slight wound. Efim grit his teeth and groaned.

"He'll go after Katya next."

"Why should I care about her? She betrayed me."

"You should care. Besides, he made her do it. He told her he would put her in a whore house."

"She is not my problem." Valery inserted the knife again on Efim's other arm and dragged it down to his hand slow and with ease.

"She can help you get to Misha." Efim nearly suffocated on his own words as he spoke, more blood rising up out of his mouth.

Valery dragged on the ritual over hours, making sure that Efim stayed conscious through the entire procedure. As the sun began to

146

poke its rays through the window Valery dropped a flap of skin onto the ground, ignoring the exposed muscle which it had covered. Efim's chest was covered with blood and vomit. Urine and feces lay in a pile under his feet.

Valery opened the barn doors and led Arina outside to the pasture. He stopped and inhaled the crisp morning air, washing the dark stains from his hands in the snow before returning to the barn.

"Are you still with me, Efim?" he asked, flicking snow at Efim's naked and exposed body.

Efim's eyes cracked open as he looked down where Valery stood before him as stoic as ever. "I...should never... Who was she? The woman."

"She was the mother of my child."

Valery's cold hand grab hold of Efim's testicles and he squeezed. Efim's eyes burst open, his body shaking uncontrollably as Valery raised his knife, finally letting the organ drop to the ground. He grabbed the glowing piece of iron from the barn stove and shoved it at the wound to stop the bleeding.

Efim's screams echoed across the farmyard, from the woods rose the replying howl of a wolf.

The following evening Valery finally walked out of the barn, leaving the stripped carcass hanging from the rafters in effigy to Jesus.

He washed the stains from his hands and entered the house. As he glanced at Svetlana's lifeless body a sadness tore through his chest. His knees gave way and he crawled over to her, gathering her up in his arms. He pressed his face into her hair, inhaling her sweet scent.

"God has forsaken me, Liybimaya." His hand slid over her belly, holding it there a moment before he finally got up from the floor.

Huddled over the kitchen stove, Valery melted a chunk of rubber from the sole of a boot in a pot while stirring in some ash from the fireplace. Using a sewing needle and the melted concoction, he began to tattoo a second dagger onto his finger through the crown.

Part Six

A Saint

Chapter Twenty

The next morning he packed a satchel with a few goods and rode Arina into the village, passing by the smoldering remains of Andrei and Olga's farm as he went. At the market he sold Arina to a nice family.

It took him a few hours walking through the countryside to finally locate the small side road in the woods. By late afternoon he had finally located the grey car he hid there, what seemed like a lifetime ago. He cleared the snow away, cranked open the door and sat inside the vehicle. His breath rose in large puffs of white in front of his face. His gloved hands gripped the steering wheel as he stared at the brown and tan interior of the car.

He glanced up at his face in the rear view mirror, his eyes slightly puffy and dark. Their normal icy grey color suddenly replaced by something more sinister.

He turned the key and the engine roared to life. It was a long drive to Kazan where he was able to find a man who ran a local factory willing to buy the car. It was easy, the car was a status symbol. Nobody asked questions about where it came from, it was best not to know.

From Kazan, Valery took the train to Zvenigorod on the western outskirts of Moscow. The snows had melted there. It was early in the morning as he walked up the small hill leading to the Savvino-Storozhevsky Monastery's white walled enclosure. The main tower stood open, but as he stepped inside a man moved within the shadows and stopped him.

"Can I help you Comrade?"

"I'm here to see Father Ivanov."

The man stepped into the light, dressed in a long black garment from head to toe. A long grey and white beard flowed down his chest. A monk from the monastery perhaps. "Follow me," he replied.

They continued through the tower and into the monastery's enclosure. Following a worn path, they made their way to a building which reminded him of St. Basil's in Moscow, though it had no colourful domes. The paint was faded and the walls were damaged, it had been ransacked and abandoned at one time. They entered the stark interior, through a short hallway and up a set of stairs, finally stopping outside a tattered wooden door.

The man raised his hand and rapped against the wood softly.

"Yes," came the reply from within. Valery recognized the voice immediately and pushed opened the door.

"Father Ivanov?" He poked his head inside and spied the old man hunched over a table, a large book lay open before him.

When the old man turned, his eyes squinting through the dim light of the room. He shifted his entire body to get a better look and finally stood. He took two careful steps forward, stopping in front of Valery. "Is it you?"

"Yes."

Father Ivanov motioned to the other man, who quietly shut the door as he left.

"Come, sit down. You are looking good."

"Not as good as I would like. I…" A lump formed in Valery's throat blocking his words. He sat on the edge of the small bed in the corner of the room as Father Ivanov moved his chair closer.

"What happened?"

"I don't want to be this way anymore, Father. I tried to live as you said. I was a good man. I met a woman, she told me I was a good man, and God took her from me. They took her from me. *He*, took her from me. And now all I can think about is making them pay for what they took from me."

Father Ivanov inhaled long and slow as he reached out his hand to Valery's knee. "Sometimes God challenges our faith to see if we are truly ready for salvation. If we believe. This is that moment, Valery. It's not up to God to believe that you are a good man, it's up to you."

"You told me once that God forgives us our sins because as his children we don't know any better."

"That's right."

"But what if we do know better? What if we know it's wrong, but we do it anyway?"

Father Ivanov leaned back in his chair and allowed his eyes to drift towards the small window. "The world is changing. So many things are changing. We are all animals, Valery, just trying to survive in the wild."

"God has forsaken me," Valery said leaning forward to rest his forearms on his legs.

Father Ivanov placed his hand on Valery's drooping head. "God has forsaken us all, my son."

The two men walked the monastery grounds, feeling the warm caress of the sun on their skin. A cool breeze drifted across their faces. Puffs of clouds floated lazily across the sky. Birds chirped in the trees outside the monastery walls.

"Russia is a country of paranoia and secrets, Valery. She's in pain. Sometimes I think I envy you."

Valery's brows creased together. "There is nothing to envy, I can assure you. It's you I should envy."

"But you don't."

They paused a moment and Valery glanced around at the six towers built into the monastery walls. "I don't. This monastery is just another prison."

"Perhaps." They continued across the grass towards the main white cathedral with its golden dome.

"I never took pleasure in what I've had to do over the years, Father."

"Even the wolf does not take pleasure in chasing down its prey. It is survival. We are all just trying to survive."

They entered the cathedral and slid into a pew, the walls absorbing any sounds they made. They sat in silence a few moments, calm and at peace, as they observed the now naked and pillaged walls around them, only a few golden frescoes remained.

"Why have you come, Valery?" Father Ivanov finally asked.

"I came to confess, Father, for I have sinned. This will be my last confession." Valery's eyes rested on the wooden cross which hung at the front of the cathedral.

"You can still walk away from it all."

"I can't. I can never walk away." Valery looked down at the tattoos on his hands. "I used think my tattoos were a symbol of who I was as a man. And because of them people left me alone. But I understand what they are now, they are my walls. My prison. They have kept me obedient. And they have made it so that I am always in the sights of the hunter, and he will never take his aim from me. Hunt or be hunted, and I must be the hunter if I am to survive."

"Even Jesus knew that one of his own would betray him. And still he did nothing."

"I am not Jesus, and I am not Judas. I am the unnamed Roman soldier who pierced Jesus on the cross. Condemned every night to my cave where I am mauled by a great lion, but by dawn I am healed. And the cycle repeats, day after day. There is no end to my suffering, Father."

"It's what you choose to do with the time that have when you are not in the cave that matters. Even while in prison you took pity on this old man. You didn't have to spare my life, but yet you did. Why?"

Valery inhaled and exhaled long and slow, his eyes dropping to his hands in his lap. "I guess I just began to wonder what the point of it all was. I realized that what they thought of me was more powerful than what I did."

"Yes, fear is a powerful weapon."

"I lost all reason to fear years ago."

"You have become the hunter."

"Like you said, Father, it's about what I choose to do with the time when I am not in the cave. But I'm not just the hunter, I am also the lion."

"Even the unnamed Roman soldier became a Saint."

Valery chuckled under his breath. "I'm not dead yet, Father."

Father Ivanov chuckled in response. "No, not yet." He gave Valery's shoulder a squeeze. "Come, you must be hungry."

They made their way to another building next to the main belfry where a handful of monks had prepared some bread, meat and cheese. As Valery removed his gloves they eyed his hands, retreating to a nearby table to eat. He grabbed a plate and began to fill it with food before following Father Ivanov onto the steps outside to eat.

"You can stay here for as long as you like. We could use someone big and strong to help us rebuild," Father Ivanov said, watching Valery's stoic face.

"I don't think so, Father." He shoved a piece of meat into his mouth.

"What's the hurry? That spear you've been carrying must be heavy. Jesus isn't going anywhere, he's nailed to the cross, remember?"

Valery chuckled.

"You will have a roof over your head, food in your belly. No one knows you're here, right?"

"No, no one knows."

"Then stay, it would make this old man happy to be able to repay you for all the kindness you have shown me."

Valery gave Father Ivanov a sideways glance as he chewed. "You're going to ruin my reputation." A smile creased his mouth.

"The Beast of Russia. As long as you are alive this country will never sleep for fear that you may be lurking in the shadows. That is the power you hold, so much so, that I bet even the ministers in Moscow continue to watch their backs."

Valery chuckled. "Father Ivanov, the tamer of beasts."

Father Ivanov slapped his knee as he laughed. "And without even a scratch."

Chapter Twenty-One

Valery walked Father Ivanov back to his room, the midday sun scattering the dark shadows from the corners of the buildings.

"This old man needs to nap. There is a room there at the end of the hall, you can use that room for as long as you stay."

"Thank you, Father."

Valery wandered the grounds within the monastery walls inspecting the destruction which the Bolsheviks had caused so many years ago when they violently looted and pillaged it. Bullet holes scarred cracked and weathered plaster. It was a tired and sad vestige of its once former regal self.

Through broken windows, Valery caught sight of something moving within the top floor of a large building at the rear of the monastery. A shadow moved through a room and then disappeared.

He stood in the doorway, his eyes scanning the deserted interior. Paint peeled from the walls. Leaves, twigs, and dirt had drifted in through the open windows. Valery listened to the stillness inside. As he stepped forward he thought he heard a child's laughter for just a moment, his body froze as he tilted his ear up to see if it was real.

Nothing.

He took a few more steps inside towards the rear of the building, bypassing the stairs. A door sat ajar, the hinges moaned as he pulled the door open further to reveal stairs which led down into the basement. As he began to push it closed more laughter echoed briefly up to him; he stood motionless staring at the darkness below.

His breathing shallowed as he strained to listen to the shadows. Small feet slapped against a thick floor. "Hello?" His voice echoed and then was quickly swallowed up by the black void.

"Hello."

Valery tensed, his hand gripping the door tighter as he pulled himself back to locate the source of the feminine voice which he had heard. Towards the front of the building at the base of the stairs stood a young woman, she was small and thin, delicate. Her long brown hair shrouded the right side of her face. She wore a plain dull grey dress, a cream sweater was loosely slung over her body.

The two of them stared at each other in silence. Sunlight streamed through the front door in a wide beam and enveloped her in a golden halo.

"I'm Lada," she finally said. Her voice had a pureness to it. A melodic innocence. "Are you lost?"

"No," Valery managed to reply as he returned the door to its former position when he had found it. "My name is Valery, I am a friend of Father Ivanov."

Staccato beating from behind the door burst it open and a young girl ran smack into his leg. Lada gasped as Valery reached down and grasped the girl's arm to steady her. The sunlight shimmered off the girl's light brown hair which hung in disarray over her shoulders. The thumping of small feet up wooden steps followed by the emergence of a little boy behind her. Both children appeared to be around six years old. When the boy looked up and saw Valery at the top of the stairs he froze in place, staring up at the giant before him.

"This is Yulia," Lada said. "And that is Oleg."

"Do you live here?" Valery asked, turning his attention back to her.

"Yes, Father Ivanov has allowed an orphanage." Lada turned her attention to the children. "Why don't you two go outside and play."

The young girl yanked her arm free from Valery and the two children padded past them and out the front door.

"I'm sorry, everything is a game to them." A pleasant smile creased her lips as Lada watched them run across the grass outside. As she turned back to Valery the sun cast a brief glow over her face revealing what appeared to be severe scarring on the right side, before her hair covered it back up.

"I've only just arrived," Valery commented.

"We've been here about a week. I remember my parents telling me about this monastery when I was a child, so when we lost our home it was the only place I could think of to bring the children. Will you be staying long?"

Valery blinked, then looked past her at the monastery outside before finally returning his gaze to her. "Yes, I have agreed to help Father Ivanov rebuild."

Yulia squealed in the distance and Lada quickly turned around to check on the children who were continuing to run around outside. When she turned back to him her eyes glanced towards his hand still holding the door. "How do you know Father Ivanov?"

Valery removed his hand and shoved them both in the pockets of his coat. "We met in prison."

"Excuse me," she said before turning and walking out of the building and towards the children. Valery watched as they continued across the monastery grounds and disappeared behind another building.

Valery sat staring at his bowl of watered down potato soup with chunks of fatty meat bobbing inside. Using his spoon, he scooped some soup and meat onto a piece of thick dry bread and took a bite.

Father Ivanov sat down across from him. "You have an orphanage here?"

"Ah, you must have met Lada and the children." Father Ivanov began to tear pieces of bread and drop them into the soup. "Have you thought about my offer to stay?"

"Yes." Valery sat forward, his arms circling around his bowl. "There is a lot of work to be done around here, it would be rude not to help. At least, until it's time for me to go."

Over the next couple weeks Valery worked hard to clear out a few old rooms in the Tsaritsa's chambers for Lada and the children. The plaster on the walls was patched up over the remains of elegantly painted designs. Broken windows were replaced with unbroken ones he had taken from other rooms. Bed mattresses were pounded clean and blankets were retrieved from the monks.

As the days became warmer he continued to work outside. The garden he and Father Ivanov planted was beginning to produce. Father Ivanov even taught Valery how to fish in the Moskva River nearby.

As Valery patched up the exterior of a wall, Lada and the children sat in the grass, hot sun beat down on them. He watched out of the corner of his eye as she read to them and cheerfully chatted. When they finally left he removed his sweat drenched shirt, savouring the slight breezed which caressed his skin.

He dipped a cup into a bucket of water and brought it to his lips as Lada emerged from around the corner of the building. Immediately she froze, staring at him like a stunned deer. Valery could almost feel her eyes drift over his body, taking in his ink stained skin.

"I...I just wanted to thank you for fixing up those rooms for us," she finally managed to say.

Valery gave a curt nod in her direction.

She opened up mouth again as if to speak but then promptly closed it. Averting her eyes, she quickly disappeared in the direction she had come from.

That evening there was a light knock on Valery's door, as he looked up it opened and Father Ivanov stepped in. "I just wanted to see how you were doing."

"We're running low on some supplies, but I think I'll have enough to finish the main building."

"I meant you. Lada tells me she ran into you today outside."

"I think I frighten her."

"No, I think you confuse her. You should talk to her, it will be good for you. You need to make friends, Valya. This old man won't be around forever."

"Nobody here is safe if I stay."

"One day you will see that you are wrong."

Valery's heavy boots thumped down the empty hallway towards the rooms which Lada and the children stayed. As he got to the door it opened. Lada stared up at him holding a broom in her hands.

"I brought wood for the stove."

She stepped aside and let him enter. He placed the small bundle of wood next to the stove. When he stood and turned around he found her staring at him, frozen next to the door. "I'm sorry if I frightened you the other day."

Lada turned her head away from him, her hair now masking her entire face where it fell. Valery stepped towards her and paused, he could see her body begin to tremble as he raised his hand and gently

160

pushed the hair from her face, revealing the scar she was hiding. "I try and cover up my past too."

"You're a Vor." Her voice was weak.

"I was."

She turned her face towards him, staring at his chest. "Father Ivanov said you saved his life."

"I think he saved mine more than he will ever take credit for."

Her eyes rose up to meet his. "Thank you, for the wood."

Valery inhaled long and slow, gave a curt nod, and walked out of the room.

Valery's feet thumped heavy on the steps, the wood creaking under his weight. The air grew cool in the darkness. A faint glow of light drifted through the opaque window spattered with mud. The bucket full of tools felt heavy in his hand as he set it down. He stared at the boiler tank before finally kneeling down before it and pulling out a wrench. One by one he began to inspect all the pipes which snaked their way from the boiler up and across the basement ceiling.

Once he was sure everything appeared to be in good working condition he returned to the boiler tank to assess the pressure valves. Sitting on a small block of wood, he held a screwdriver in his hand and stared at the panel, unsure what to do next.

"What are you doing?"

Valery's heart thumped rapidly in his chest, the screwdriver falling to the floor as Yulia stepped forward into the light from the window. His fist clenched as he calmed himself and retrieved the screwdriver. "I'm fixing this boiler so that we can heat the belfry. It'll be fall soon."

"Is that your job?" she asked, brushing her small fingers across the boiler's surface.

"To fix things?"

She nodded.

He thought about it a moment before replying, "Yes."

She stepped up next to him and placed her hand on his shoulder. The weight of it barely noticeable, yet endearing and comforting. "Can I help?"

Valery glanced up at her round face. "I'm done. But you can help me carry my tools out."

Her lips pressed into a smile as he handed her the wrench that was next to his foot. Obediently she followed him out of the basement and outside.

He stopped at the front door and looked around for any signs of Lada or Oleg, but the yard was empty. Yulia slid her hand into Valery's, her tiny fingers grasping his as tight as they could. His body stiffened and his throat tightened. "Where is Oleg?" He looked down at Yulia who shrugged her shoulders.

"He was chasing squirrels." Her eyes focused on his hand holding her own. "You have pictures." She raised her other hand and realized she was still holding the wrench so lifted it up for Valery to take. Her fingers began to trace the patterns on his fingers. "Why do you have pictures on your hands?"

"Yulia, come help me," Lada said as she walked towards the two of them.

Valery felt his body relax as Yulia let go of his hand and ran towards Lada. He watched as they walked away, noticing that Lada now had her hair swept away from her face.

Chapter Twenty-Two

Valery awoke early and headed towards the river to fish. Rising hues of sunlight reflect off the surface of the water. He set his fishing gear down and lifted his shirt over his head before kicking off his boots as he undid his pants. Once free of all his clothing he stepped forward into the cool water. He dipped his head under, then smoothed his hair back off his face.

When he opened his eyes he noticed a man a short ways down the embankment watching him. The man remained still, the two men watching each other. Slowly Valery began to step out of the water, each step revealing more of the tattoos on his body. The man down the embankment remained still, unmoved by what he saw. Valery faced the man directly as he began to dress, watching for any signs that the man either recognized him or showed signs of fear, but there was nothing.

Only when he was finally completely dressed did the man begin to walk away. Valery gathered up his gear and walked in the direction the man had went but was unable to locate him. There was no way to know if he was Vor or State Security, either option was not favourable. After circling back around the area, sure that he wasn't being followed, he made his way back to the monastery.

During breakfast Valery stared at the bowl of cabbage soup in front of him.

"You are more quiet than usual this morning," Father Ivanov noted.

Valery glanced up at him across the table. "I saw a man by the river this morning."

"A villager?"

163

"He was watching me." Valery sighed, pressing both his hands flat against the table. "I was stupid. I had removed my clothing and gone into the water."

"You think he recognized you?"

Valery clasped his hands under his chin. "I don't know. The State has spies everywhere. I should not have stayed, I've put everyone here in danger."

"No. If it was a spy then they won't act unless you give them a reason to."

"What if someone in here has told them about me?"

"They would never do that. The last thing we want is for the police to come and raid us again. As long as we keep to ourselves they leave us alone."

"Even so… I will move to the abandoned building in the far corner of the grounds just in case."

Father Ivanov nodded as he watched Valery's face for any sign of concern, but the man remained stoic.

Valery lay on the thin mattress on the floor listening to the sounds of the night through the broken windows as they drifted in on a cool breeze. An owl called out in the distance. He shifted on the mattress, bringing his focus to the lamp at his side, his eyes watching the flame dance within.

A floorboard squeaked, quickly he sat up, his eyes directed at the doorway. His hand slid to the knife under his pillow as a shadow moved in the hallway coming towards him. Slowly the figure came into view.

"Lada? What are you doing here?" His hand released its hold on the knife and slid back to his side. "Are the children okay?"

She stopped in the doorway, her hands clutching the shawl wrapped tightly around her shoulders. "I saw the light from my room. I couldn't sleep." She stepped forward and knelt next to him, letting the shawl slide from her shoulders to reveal a very thin nightgown underneath.

Valery's eyes dropped to her exposed shoulders. "What are you doing?"

"I know men like you get lonely. I...just wanted to thank you for everything you've done."

Valery reached out and pulled the shawl back up. "You don't need to thank me like this."

Lada trembled, a tear sliding down her cheek. "I just thought…"

Valery brushed her tear away with his thumb. "I'm not that kind of man." Lada raised her hand to cover the scar on the side of her face. "No, it's not that." Her brows creased together and Valery chuckled. "No, not that either." Her face relaxed, a small smile across her lips.

"Don't you ever get lonely?"

Valery brought his legs up and rested his arms on his knees. "People near me tend to end up hurt. It's safer to be alone."

"You frighten me. You did. But then I realized that I was looking at you the way most people look at me."

"How did it happen?" he asked, directing his gaze at her scars.

"My family lived near Smolensk when the Germans attacked. I was thirteen at the time. They destroyed our village, I was trapped in our house as it burned. Someone heard my screams and managed to pull me out, but my parents had already died. We were evacuated to Moscow and I was later sent to an orphanage."

"I lost my parents when I was young too."

They sat in silence, time slowing. Lada stared at her fingers as she spoke. "What do your tattoos mean?"

It was a question no one had ever asked Valery before. In his world, everyone knew what they meant. His thumb rubbed over the ring tattoo on his hand, a circle with a black dot in the center. "This one means I was an orphan."

"Have you killed people?"

Valery looked up and met Lada's eyes before giving a slight nod.

"Did they deserve to die?"

"Yes."

A smile coyly crossed Lada's face. "This children call you the Painted Man."

Valery cocked an eyebrow at her. "The Painted Man?"

"Because of your tattoos. They think you were a circus performer."

Valery chuckled. "I have never seen the circus."

Lada's smile widened. "Neither have they. I used to tell them stories about when I was a little girl. I saw the circus once, they had clowns."

"They think I am a clown?"

Lada burst into laughter. Valery watched her expression, the mirth softening his stoic features, causing him to join her.

Her eyes sparkled as she watched him. "I don't think I've ever seen you smile before."

Valery's smile quickly faded.

Lada's laughter became stifled, her face growing serious. "Does anything frighten you?"

His eyes shifted to the lamp. "No."

"You're not afraid to die?"

"I died years ago."

"I should return to the children." Lada stood and walked towards the door.

"Lada," Valery said, causing her to stop. "Do I still frighten you?"

Her gaze drifted along the floor before finally coming up to meet his. "Should I be?" Before giving him a chance to answer, she disappeared into the shadows.

Valery tossed and turned for the next few hours before finally deciding that he needed some air. He headed outside and began to walk along the perimeter of the monastery. The night was cool, the sky clear, allowing the stars to shine brightly. The moon was nearly full. Fall was creeping in.

He had been at the monastery for nearly six months already. He had lost track of time, and not once been tempted to return to Moscow and find Mikhail as he had intended. He had found a freedom within the monastery walls which he actually enjoyed.

Valery entered the cathedral and walked between the pews until he was staring up at the worn wooden cross hanging above him. For the first time in his life he knelt before it, clasped his hands and pressed them to his forehead, and began to pray.

Somewhere around him he could hear the routine of life as monks entered the cathedral to say their morning prayers. Sometime later they left and he was alone again. He could feel another presence enter and walk up behind him. They stopped and remained there until Valery forgot they existed. Finally he heard the feet moving around him until a shadow cast over him. And as the strong fingers touched the top of his head the bubble of emotion he had been repressing his entire life burst.

Tears streamed down Valery's face as he began to gasp, trying desperately to choke them back. The pain in his knees from kneeling on the hard wood floor vanished. And in time everything else subsided, until a calm began to settle into him again. He wiped his face and finally looked up.

Father Ivanov looked down. "You are forgiven, Valery."

Valery nodded, wiping his face one last time before finally rising to his feet. "I want to devote my life to the church, Father. I want to become a priest."

"A life devoted to the church is no easy task, Valery. It has its own challenges, but I will not deny you this if it is truly what you seek."

"It is Father. I need a purpose. For most of my life my purpose was to hurt people and to kill. I need a stronger purpose. I want to help people, Father."

"You already have been. You don't need the church to do that."

"I know."

"Very well, come with me."

Valery moved back into the room down the hall from Father Ivanaov's, and for the next three months he stayed there. Taking a vow of silence, he spent his days in prayer and reading the bible. The monks brought him food, cleared out his waste bucket and brought fresh water for him to wash. On sunny days he could hear the children playing outside, but soon the weather became cold and their laughter became less frequent.

There came a soft knock on his door before it opened. Valery remained where he sat on his bed next to the window as he read the bible. When he looked up, Father Ivanov stood silently waiting. Valery nodded and he entered the room.

"Tomorrow is the Presentation of Theotokos. I should like for you to join us for the ceremony. There will be a feast after."

Valery's gaze dropped back to the open book in his hands.

"You can't hide up here forever. Your vow of silence has been fulfilled." At that Father Ivanov left.

The next morning Valery dressed in the long black cassock that had been left for him, and carefully placed the skufia on his head. He caught sight of his reflection in the window, the dark beard on his face causing his silvery grey eyes to stare out vibrantly in contrast. A long gold chain and cross lay flat against his chest, resting snuggly at the base of his sternum.

Valery kept to the back rooms of the cathedral as he prepared for the ceremony with the monks, rehearsing his duties and memorizing the prayers. When he finally stepped into the nave of the cathedral his body tensed at the sight of so many people. Nearly twenty locals from the surrounding villages had shown up.

Lada and the children sat off to the rear, he could see the look of excitement on their faces as he walked past. Lada tried desperately to subdue them and get them to remain still. He took his seat at the front of the nave with the monks as they waited for Father Ivanov to address everyone. His eyes began to scan the faces of the crowd and his body began to relax.

As Father Ivanov began to speak Valery found it impossible to concentrate, his mind drifting in and out of the present. "And now I would like to call on Valery to come and read to you about the

Presentation of Theotokos so that we may all remember why we are here."

Valery's eyes snapped back over to Father Ivanov, a lump formed in Valery's throat as he stood. His heart beat loud in his ears as he rose from his seat and slowly stepped forward. Father Ivanov greeted him with a reassuring hand on his arm before stepping aside. Keeping his eyes on the pages before him, Valery began to read. The cathedral was silent as he spoke. Then finally, as the last line left his lips he allowed himself to raise his eyes. His breath caught in his throat and his muscles tensed as a familiar face stared back at him from the audience.

Chapter Twenty-Three

Valery kept his eyes focused on Father Ivanov until the end of service, but his mind was everywhere other than in church. When the service finished he quickly slipped out of the cathedral and headed over to the small refectory to prepare for the feast. He knew he would not be able to escape that face forever, but he needed more time.

As people began filing into the dining hall Valery watched from the farthest corner he could find. It was not too far for the children to find him and rush over, the word "Father" on their lips. He knelt down to embrace them, their excitement bringing temporary relief from his dark thoughts.

He rose to his feet to greet Lada. "The children missed you very much." Her eyes took in his features. "You look so different with a beard."

"I'm still getting used to it," he said as his hand gave it a little tug.

"It suits you, I think." She smiled. "Will you eat with us? I know the children have so much to tell you."

He gave her a curt nod and they walked away to claim their plates of food from the monks. Valery hung back, but soon regretted it as that familiar face peered at him through the crowd of people. His hands clenched into fists at his sides as she approached. Quickly he scanned the room for signs of anyone else he may recognize, finally landing back on her as she stopped in front of him.

"I'm not sure how I should address you. Father?" An eyebrow raised in question as she held his gaze.

"I have not yet taken my full vows, you can address me however you wish, Katya."

"I nearly didn't recognize you. So this is where you've come to hide."

"I am not hiding."

"Yes, this close to Moscow someone was bound to find you." A smile splayed out across her face.

"What are you doing here?" His body remained rigid, his eyes frozen on her face.

"Were you ever going to tell me?"

"Tell you what?"

"About your family?"

Valery's brows creased. "Family?"

"The woman in the red dress."

Valery's eyes scanned the room, but he was unable to see any woman in a red dress. He brought his eyes back to Kaya. "I don't know what you're talking about."

"The woman in the red dress with the two children. I heard them call you father."

Valery could hardly stifle his chuckle, his face relaxing. "They are orphans who live in the monastery. And as you can see, I have become a Father."

The anger slid from her face, pink spreading out across her cheeks.

"You should leave." Valery turned away, but her hand reached out and grabbed his arm.

"I'm sorry, I didn't come here to argue with you. I just wanted to see you again."

"I forgive you, Katya. That is what you want to hear, no? Please leave me alone."

Tears began to well in her eyes. "Valya, please. I…" Her throat became dry and sticky as she forced herself to swallow. Valery gently removed her hand from his arm. "I need your help."

"That's not my world anymore, Kat. This is my world now."

"Please, just meet me down by the river tomorrow at dawn."

"I refuse to listen to your lies anymore. Go."

"Please, at dawn. I know you don't trust me. But please, Valya. There is something I need to show you."

"If I agree, will you promise to never come here again?"

"I will do whatever you ask."

"Very well." Calmly he walked away, leaving Katya behind as he joined the monks and began to serve food.

When he sat down with Lada and the children to finally eat he was relieved at the distraction they brought. Oleg couldn't wait to show Valery the small wooden bear he had found in the village. Yulia crawled onto his lap and threw her arms around his neck, telling him stories about all their adventures over the past few months. Lada laughed at their antics trying to calm them down.

Valery stared at Lada unable to get something Katya said out of his mind. The woman in the red dress. Only, he had never seen Lada wear a red dress, it was always the same pale grey with a cream colored sweater.

Lada caught his gaze. "What is it?"

"Nothing." He forced his mouth into a smile. "You've done something different with your hair."

A blush washed over her face as her hand reached back to touch the hair piled on the back of her head.

"It looks good," he added, before turning his attention back to the children.

The night would not bring him sleep as he tossed and turned in his bed, spending much of it staring out the window at the clouds drifting past the moon. Just as he had thought he had finally left his past behind him, in it walked. It was possible that Katya was setting him up again, but he resigned that he would take whatever punishment God gave him.

When the sun began to creep over the horizon he slid from bed, knelt before the small cross on the wall to say one last prayer before heading out. The grass was wet with dew, the moisture clinging to his cassock and weighing it down with each step towards the river. He spotted Katya right away between the trees, but took his time scouting the area before finally approaching.

"Katya," he said, stepping forward. When she turned around the colour drained from his face. In her arms she clutched a small child bundled in a blanket. He opened his mouth to speak, but was unable to utter a sound.

"This is Valentina Valeryevna Nikitinova. She is your daughter, Valya."

He stood motionless staring at the small child in her arms. "How can that be?"

"After you were sent to prison I found out I was pregnant. You were the only man I have ever been with, Valya. She is yours."

His hands fisted at his sides, his body rigid. "No."

"It was hard to conceal the pregnancy from Misha, but luckily the winter was long and I was able to cover it up with sweaters and a jacket."

"Why are you doing this, Kat? Why now?" He inhaled long and deep, releasing the breath slowly. A trail of vapor drifted up in front of his face.

"You know as well as I that there are always eyes watching, Valya. When I heard you were out here I was elated. Then I was terrified, I thought maybe you had come back to…" She paused using her finger to pull the blanket down from the child's face so Valery could see her clearly. "She's getting bigger by the day and I won't be able to keep her hidden from Misha for much longer. If he finds out she's yours I'm afraid of what he might do."

"How am I to protect her? How am I supposed to take care of a baby, Kat?"

"You said the monastery has an orphanage. If she is here with you I know she will be safe. Please."

"A child should be with its mother."

Tears began to trickle down Katya's cheeks, each panicked breath clouding her face. "Please Valya. Please protect our daughter. I know you are probably still mad at me for what happened, but please don't take it out on her. All I want is for her to have a good life. A better life than I can give her."

"What do you mean than you can give her? You have an education, get a job with the government, that's what Misha paid for, isn't it?" Valery could feel an anger begin to rise up from his gut, but he pushed it back down as he had always done. *"Emotion is weakness, Valya. Never let them see what's going on inside,"* Misha had told him as a boy.

"Yes, but… Please take her, Valya."

Valery exhaled long and slow. "Tell me the truth. Why should I take her?"

She shifted the sleepy child in her arms. "Misha has arranged a marriage for me to a commissar. If they find out about the baby..."

Valery raised his hand to silence her. He reached out his arms and took the child from her, cradling it snuggly against his chest. "I don't ever want to see you here again, do you understand?"

Katya nodded, wiping the tears from her face. Her hand reached towards the child one last time. Valery stepped back. The expression on her face fell away in shock.

"Stay away, Katya. Don't ever come back here. If you do, I won't be able to protect her."

She nodded solemnly, tears streaming down her cheeks as Valery turned away and headed back to the monastery.

Swollen drops began to fall from the grey clouds which had moved in low in the sky. Each one burst on Valery's face, masking the tears streaming down his cheeks, his body trembling more with each step. As he got inside the safety of the monastery walls he stopped, staring up at the sky above as he clutched the child close. He wanted desperately to shout, to roar at God for all the deception, but could only hold the child closer.

Water pooled at his feet when he finally stepped into the refectory. Lada spotted him across the room and quickly leapt from her seat. As he sat down she threw her shawl over his shoulders and knelt before him. Her hands reached up towards the bundle in his arms which was beginning to wake.

"What happened?" Gently she pulled down the side of the blanket to reveal the child's face, bright silvery grey eyes looked back at her.

Water dripped from Valery's nose as his arms began to relax and he looked down at the child.

"Whose child is this?" Lada asked as she wiped the rain from the child's face.

Valery could barely force the words past the lump in his throat. "She's mine."

Lada looked up at him in shock. "Yours? How?"

"From another life."

"The woman yesterday."

Valery nodded.

The child began to whimper and squirm, just on the edge of crying. Lada reached forward to try and retrieve her from Valery's firm hold. "Let me take her, she must be hungry. What's her name?"

"Valentina."

"She takes after her father. It's okay," she said, coaxing Valery to release his hold. "Go dry off and change, we'll wait here for you."

Valery nodded, watching Lada walk away with the child.

His hands clenched at his sides as he made his way towards his room, nearly bumping into Father Ivanov in the hallway. Father Ivanov looked Valery up and down slowly. "What happened?"

Valery brushed passed him. "I need to change."

Father Ivanov followed him back to his room. "I can sense an anger in you, Valery. You must not let it fester."

Valery groaned as he tore his cassock over his head and began to unbutton the shirt he had on underneath it. He threw the garments over the back of the chair before grabbing dry ones from a small cupboard nearby. Father Ivanov watched him, patiently waiting for him to speak.

Once dressed, Valery sat down on the end of his bed, bent over, resting his head in his hands. "Every time I think I'm finally free of my past, it sucks me back in, Father."

Father Ivanov rested his hand on Valery's shoulder. "You have carried a heavy burden for so long."

"I have a daughter," he finally grumbled.

Father Ivanov gave Valery's shoulder a slight squeeze. "Congratulations."

"What am I going to do?"

"The mother is not caring for the child?"

Valery raised his head. "She can't. If the Pakhan finds out about her, he'll have her killed." He paused a moment. "Because she's mine."

"She is here now?"

Valery nodded.

"Then she is safe. And she is in the care of her father. That is a wonderful gift God has given you."

Valery's brows furrowed. "Before I arrived here I had a woman. We lived on a farm. She was pregnant with my child. I thought I may actually be happy having a family. Yet when she died I felt relieved."

"You weren't ready yet."

"How do you know when you're ready? I think about my own father who was never around, and when he was he was drunk."

"You're ready now, Valery."

"How do you know?"

"Because God would not have brought her to you if you weren't."

Chapter Twenty-Four

Lada insisted on taking care of Valentina during the day while Valery performed his duties at the monastery. Often he would stop and watch the children playing in their rooms. With each day he became more accustomed to his new role. Life began to take on more of a routine, less tension and apprehension. It was almost as if he was looking forward to the future and this new life he had created.

Valentina wobbled on unsure legs as she crossed the floor towards him, he scooped her into his arms and walked over to the window where they watched the large white flakes of snow fall to the ground. Her small fingers jabbed at the window as she giggled.

Out of the corner of his eye Valery was sure he saw a figure step out from behind a tree just outside the monastery walls and then retreat back behind it. He studied the area but couldn't see any signs of a person. His eyes remained transfixed for a time until Valentina began to squirm, demanding to be set down.

When he stood back up he could see the dark figure retreating further into the trees. It was definitely male, skinny, average height. Perhaps a young boy from the village.

"I'll see you all at dinner," he said as he walked out of the room.

Valery crossed the grounds, pulling the collar of his coat up around his neck and shoving his hands in his pockets. His eyes were so set on the monastery's main gate tower that he didn't see Father Ivanov approaching him from the cathedral on the right.

"Valya!" he finally heard and stopped, turning to greet Father Ivanov. "Where are you off to in such a hurry?"

Valery glanced over to the tower. "Nowhere."

"If you have a moment, I wanted to speak to you about your vows."

Valery gave a curt nod and the two men headed back to the monastery's belfry.

"Patriarch Alexy has arranged for you to perform your vows in the New Year, if this is still what you want?"

"Yes, of course."

"There is one thing you should consider. If you are married before you take your vows you will not be required to take a vow of celibacy. But if you aren't, you will not be permitted to marry at any time in the future."

"I understand."

"Do you?" Father Ivanov looked deep into Valery's eyes. "I am an old man, being celibate is easy. But you are still a young man, Valery."

Valery shifted his weight on his feet.

"You have a daughter now. And I've seen the way that Lada looks at you."

"Lada?" His eyes glanced back towards the residences.

"Just think about it, you've still got time."

That night after the children had gone to bed Valery found himself staring out the window at the tree tops beyond the wall. Bright moonlight lit up the snow and everything around it. Lada's feet padded softly across the floor towards him and she propped herself up against the side of window next to him.

"You've been quiet all day."

"Father Ivanov says that I will be able to take my vows in the New Year." His eyes dropped to his hand on the window sill where his finger scratched at the wood.

"That is good, yes?"

Valery sighed. "It is."

"Are you nervous?"

Valery glanced up at her. "Nervous? No. I have never been more sure about anything. This is where I belong."

Lada nodded and their eyes met, holding each other for a moment before Valery returned his to the winter landscape beyond the window. Lada began to step away when Valery spoke again. "You are no longer frightened of me." He looked at her and she gently moved her head from side to side. "If you knew of the things that I have done…"

"I don't need to know those things. That's not who you are now, Valya. I don't believe it was ever who you were."

His eyes drifted down as he considered her words.

Lada took a step towards him and reached up, her finger traced along his eyebrow and down the side of his face, causing him to lift his eyes up to hers. "You deserve to be happy, Valya."

As she removed her hand Valery suddenly grasped hold of it tightly, causing her to gasp. His other hand reached up and grasped her chin as he brought his mouth to hers. Her lips were soft and warm as they gently pressed against his. Her body relaxed into him. The moment felt too short as he finally pulled away, Lada's chest heaving, her cheeks flushed. "Good night, Lada."

Valery stepped aside and walked out of the room, pausing only long enough to grab his coat before walking out of the residences and into the night's crisp air. He continued across the grounds and through the eastern gate. Snow crunched under foot as he strode across the mound which the monastery sat atop and towards the trees. The snow clung to the length of his cassock making it difficult to walk, but he pushed his way through, the snow now midway up to his knees.

As he got within the cover of the trees he spotted the tracks. They were large, not an animal, definitely human. He began to follow them as they wove around the monastery, seeming to merge with a new set of tracks and split of again.

Hearing movement to his left he lunged to the side just as a knife took a swipe at him. His hand grabbed hold of the wrist and squeezed, pushing it away as a fist made contact with his jaw. Valery grabbed hold of the other arm and then forcefully head butted his opponent, causing the stranger to drop the knife and stumble back into the snow.

The man wore a balaclava covering his face. The eyes were two small black dots on his face, they squinted as they focused on Valery and he lunged forward again, knocking the two of them back. They struggled in the snow, the stranger trying desperately to get a good punch in, but Valery was much larger and stronger than him, blocking his every attempt at a shot. Out of the corner of his eye he spotted the knife and tried to reach up for it as they continued to roll about in the snow.

Finally the masked man got a good punch in and jumped off Valery, reaching out for the knife. As Valery tried to crawl to his feet the man swung his arm around and the knife jabbed into his shoulder. Valery groaned as the pain shot through his arm and down his side. He reached up and pulled the knife free, swinging it just high enough to make contact with the stranger's throat.

The man's hands immediately clutched at his throat, gasping through wet garbles as he tried to speak.

"Who sent you?" Valery asked, kneeling over the man.

The man kicked his legs, as his hands continuing to clutch at his throat before his body finally went still.

Valery reached up to his aching shoulder as he stood. When he turned around he came face to face with a new adversary, and a gun pointed directly at his chest. The two men stared at each other, each waiting for the other to make a move.

"Saint Valya," he chuckled. "I had to come see it for myself. I didn't believe her at first. She held out longer than I thought she would, Katya. But even God can't wash all the blood from your hands."

"I have no quarrel with you, Misha."

"I heard what happened to Efim."

Valery inhaled long and slow as he straightened his posture.

"All because of a woman? They always lead to trouble, Valya."

"Why are you here?"

Misha's eyes scanned over the black garment which hung down to Valery's feet. "I really thought the girl was lying, but here you stand. The church? Do you really think God can forgive you for all that you have done?"

"Is that why you came? Forgiveness?"

Misha's hand clenched the gun tighter. "You were like a son to me, Valya. The day you betrayed me and went to work for enemy, I can never forgive you for that."

"I'm sorry you feel that way." Valery shifted on his feet in the snow, his arm going numb.

"I've had many sleepless nights thinking about you."

183

"Should I be flattered?"

"I know you, Valya. There is no way you'd rest until you stood over my dead body. And yet instead you have come to cower behind the walls of God and beg forgiveness for your sins."

"So you are here to kill me?" Valery let go of his bleeding shoulder and splayed his arms out at his sides. "Here's your chance, Misha. If it is God's will, then I deserve whatever punishment I get."

A smile slid across Mikhail's face. "Ah, you're making this too easy." He pulled the trigger and a flash erupted from the end of the gun.

Something slammed into Valery's stomach causing him to lurch back. A jolt of adrenaline surged through his veins and he lunged forward, grabbing the gun in Mikhail's hand. The two men struggled, each trying to gain control of the weapon. They stumbled in the snow, Valery falling on top of Misha as they continued to wrestle with the weapon.

With one hand Valery clutched Misha's throat, squeezing tight, his fingers curling around the other man's esophagus. The other hand restrained the hand holding the gun. Misha kicked, but didn't have the strength to move Valery's giant frame. Mikhail flailed his free hand at Valery's face, trying to grab hold of anything.

Valery pressed his body flat against Misha's, released his hold on the man's neck and clasped both hands around the gun still clutched in Misha's hand. Using all his strength he twisted it free and rolled onto his side, pointing the gun out in front of him.

Misha laughed as he sat up, hunched over. Valery could see one of his hands slide down to his boot. Quickly he pulled the trigger, the gun flashed and Misha's shoulder jerked to the side, throwing him back to the ground.

Valery crawled forward trying to reach for Misha's boot where a second gun was hidden. Just as his hand made contact with Misha's boot, Misha pulled the gun free and the barrel flashed. The sudden impact to Valery's chest caused him to fire his gun in return. Misha's body went limp.

Valery gasped, continuing to crawl forward until he could remove the gun from Misha's hand and toss it aside.

A metallic taste entered his mouth as he pushed himself to his knees. His breathing became short. He sat in the stillness listening to the wind gently blowing through the tree branches above his head. His eyes drifted to the white snow spread out like a soft blanket on the ground. Beneath him, red began to creep, staining the snow slowly.

Red. The colour of blood. His blood.

He stared at the red staining his hands, his vision blurring. In the distance someone called out to him. He blinked his eyes, trying to clear his vision as he raised his head. Somewhere in the halo of white beyond the trees a figure in red was approaching.

END.

ALSO AVAILABLE ON AMAZON

The Prophecy of Constantinople

Some prophecies bring the promise of hope and peace, others bring the terror of death and destruction. The old Gods die, only to be replaced by new Gods.

In 1453 Constantinople fell to the Ottomans, tearing down a 1,100 year old empire, and the last vestiges of the Eastern Roman Empire. Many thought it had been lost forever, but the last prophecy of Constantinople told a different story. A story with much older beginnings.

After the Chernobyl accident, Natalya became an orphan along with her twin brother. At the age of six she was taken to live in Canada, separated from her brother, never knowing what became of him. Until one day, fate brought them together and ignited the words of an ancient prophecy, forever changing history.

Prologue

Constantinople – 1453

The priest was dressed in the traditional black cassock from head to toe. Embroidered in red, the Chi-Rho sat over his heart. The wooden heals of his shoes clacked along the stone, echoing under the great dome as he walked through the cathedral which sat high on the mount. He stopped at the altar, a solemn old man dressed in a crimson cassock knelt before a gold cross.

"Pardon me, Superior General, we have received news."

The old man opened his eyes. "Speak."

"It is as you suspected, the Priesthood of Horus has joined with the Sultan and they are raising an army to come and sack the city."

The man in scarlet calmly rose to his feet. "Very well, we must prepare for the inevitable. Gather the Order and make preparations, we'll head north."

Beneath the Hagia Sophia the Superior General walked the crypts with his Cardinals. The air was cool and musky, smelling of dirt and decay. The torchlight danced across the walls bringing shadows to life, raising the souls of the dead from where they lay. They entered a large open crypt, large marble sarcophagi were on display around the perimeter, in the center of the room sat a large tomb of red stone. The figures carved into the surface seemed to dance in the flame light a macabre waltz of their impending doom.

"We knew this time would come," the Superior General said as he reached inside and pulled out an old leather-bound book with thick, coarse, dry pages. "I will go north, and each of you will spread out across Europe and to the new world in the west. Let the false gods have their city, their time is done in the world." He flipped open the book, stopping near the last page. "I will share with you the last prophecy of Constantinople to take with you. Stay ever vigilant, for the prophet's words are the language of images."

He angled the book against the torchlight and began to read. "On the eve of the invisible death, pale ghosts will rise with eyes of fire and jade. And the Old Kingdom will tremble and sorrow. Therefore behold the days that come, cast no judgement. Beware the Watchmen from the land of scorched earth for they know not what they have done. And they will look and say, behold the pale ghost, and cast out their eyes and beg forgiveness for their sins. The end times are coming and the seat of the Almighty will gaze down upon the heathens. Fear not my believers, for the dead cannot touch you, but guard your thoughts, for the ghosts of Constantinople will return and cast their judgement over you. Take heed, should their union be broken."

A young priest ran into the tomb interrupting them, gasping for each breath. "They're nearly here!"

The Superior General closed the book and looked to his brothers. "Safe travels, and may the true God be with you."

Montreal, Canada – Present Day

Father Joubert woke with a start, his heart beating against his ribs. A dim light from the street filtered through the curtains, casting a beam across the bed.

"Do you know who I am, Father?" That voice. The accent sounded familiar. The figured shifted forward slightly, the lower half of his face barely visible in the moonlight revealing thin lips spread into a muted smile which slowly faded.

"I'm sorry, I…" Father Joubert pushed himself up against the headboard.

"Once upon a time there was a priest on mission in Ukraine. And one day he came upon small village. And in that village was old orphanage. I'm sure you know this story."

"I did mission work once in Ukraine, but…"

"Now don't interrupt. So one day this sad lonely priest stumble upon this old orphanage. And in yard he sees young girl. He take pity on this girl. But she's not ordinary girl, she's special. So special that God speaks to him that day, and the old lonely priest decides he must adopt her, take her away from her home to different country."

"I'm not sure I understand."

"You took something from me, a piece of me. I want it back. Where is she?" The figure stepped from the shadows to reveal pale white skin with pale blond hair to match. Albino. Except something looked familiar about him, his eyes. One red, one green.

Father Joubert gasped. "You? But…how did you find me?"

"Did you miss me, Father?" the voice growled with distaste.

"You misunderstand me, leaving you as I did. It wasn't what you think."

190

"I'm going to find her, there's nothing you can do to stop me." Through his movements moonlight glinted off a metallic surface.

"You'll never find her. She has a good life now, she doesn't even remember you. You were a curse of the devil even as a little boy."

"A curse? I always like demon spawn, myself. But I've changed now, Father." He leaned forward, holding the knife up to Father Joubert's jaw. "I'm much worse now."

Provincial Father Valois opened the folder on his desk, the pages flopping around. "Natalya Saint Charlemagne," he said, reading the print.

"She went by Noelle," Father Arnaud corrected.

Valois's eyes shifted up. "We'd like you to locate her."

Arnaud leaned forward in his chair. "Why me?"

Provincial Father Valois picked up the picture of a teenaged Noelle, taking a closer look. "Her eyes."

"Yes, one is red. She is albino."

"Albino?" He handed the picture over to Father Arnaud. "Your plane leaves in three hours. The last communication Father Joubert received from her is this postcard shortly after she had left." He handed over the postcard. "It's postmarked from Vancouver. We have reason to believe that she may be in contact with a Detective Thomas, he's listed on a report which identifies a woman who seems to match Noelle's description. He may know where to locate her." Valois handed over the rest of the file.

Father Arnaud placed the file in his lap, his hand gently resting on it. "Your Excellency, why me?"

"She trusts you."

Arnaud shifted uneasily in his seat.

Chapter One

Vancouver, Canada – Present Day

The scent of spring blossoms saturated the air. Cherry blossom petals littered the sidewalks, a momentary speck of beauty crushed under each step Natalya took down the sidewalk. Warm rays of midday sun warmed her face from the cool breeze that still left a chill on the body. She turned onto a muddy footpath and continued through a vacant lot, finally emerging on the far side of a mall parking lot.

Out of the corner of her eye she caught sight of a man standing at the rear of his truck, the canopy hatch was open and he was holding a large industrial sized wrench in his hand, swinging down at something under the canopy. As Natalya neared she could hear the high pitched squeals.

Redirecting her course, she strolled along the edge of the lot towards a loose metal sign post, which a cataract ravaged shopper had misjudged in their haste to purchase more useless stuff from the mall and pushed up from the ground. The post sat nearly at a forty-five degree angle, the lumpy concrete base pulled up from the ground.

Natalya yanked the post free, gripping the metal pipe tightly in her small delicate hands as she continued around the rear of the truck to find that the inbred, beer soaked hillbilly with the wrench was beating a small brown and white Pit Bull, the face swollen and bloodied as it cowered against a tire.

Lifting the pipe high into the air, Natalya came to a stop behind the man. Using all her strength her small frame could muster, throwing her body weight into the swing, she brought the concrete encrusted end of pipe down on the man's head. Immediately the man collapsed, his head rebounding off the tail gate of the truck on his way down to the ground. A small pool of blood began to leak around the man's disgruntled face which lay smooshed against the pavement. As he tried to get up she stepped over him, dropped the pipe next to his head and knelt. Like magic she deftly pulled a pen from her pocket and held it securely in her hand. "God works in mysterious ways." She jabbed the tip of the pen into the man's aorta, the blood seeping from around the edges. She yanked it free, blood pumping onto the pavement as he reached up pathetically trying to stop it.

Natalya wiped the pen off on the man's shirt, shoved it back into her pocket and stood. Carefully she gathered the crying dog into her arms, tucking it into her jacket before disappearing back into the bushes of the vacant lot.

Detective Jack Thomas slowed the shaky cell phone video, watching it for the hundredth time, the image grainy, clearly depicting the dead man had been beating a small dog in the back of his truck with a wrench when a young woman approached, knocked him over the head, and took the dog. It was impossible to make out her face, although her skin was so pale it almost seemed to glow under the sun. She wore a cap pulled down, shrouding her face from view, her shoulder length hair pale blonde.

"Let it go, man. The piece of shit clearly got what he deserved." Detective Kowalski clapped his partner on the shoulder. "She did us a favour. Besides, it's been three weeks, she could be long gone by now."

"Thomas, Kowalski, get in here," Captain Harris shouted from behind the desk in his office, because clearly walking the ten feet to their desks was too much work. Kowalski grabbed his coffee while Thomas logged off his computer terminal before heading over. "Close the door."

Natalya sat quietly on the museum's soft bench as she stared up at Rodin's sculpture of *The Gates of Hell*. Much like the figure of The Thinker at the top of the sculpture, she too often felt like she was sitting, staring down on the Gates of Hell below. The world erupting into an enigmatic chaos around her.

To her left shouting erupted as a crazed man grabbed a young woman. He shouted at the onlookers. Sweat beaded across his brow, his eyes wide and panicked. The man resembled every bit the stereotype of a crazed suicide bomber. He dragged the woman closer to where Natalya was sitting, his eyes darting about sporadically before finally landing on her.

Natalya remained calm and still, watching the scene unfold in front of her like a movie. "Oh, please continue. Don't mind me, I'm just here for the sculpture," she said, motioning towards large sculpture in front of her.

The man jerked his head towards the chaotic reaching figures and then back to Natalya, where she sat calmly on the bench. "Get up!" he shouted at her.

Slowly she turned her eyes in his direction. "No, I'm not done yet."

As their eyes met, the man momentarily froze in a panic, before suddenly regaining his insanity. "Get up!" he shouted again, this time holding his victim out from him as he pointed his gun at Natalya. His jacket opened to reveal a vest of explosives.

Natalya's eyes scanned the device quickly as she stood. "I am not going to let the irrational behaviour of a confused individual who is allowing his emotions to control his actions ruin my day. So please," she splayed her hands out at her sides, "continue with what you're doing."

The man balked, confusion wrinkling his brows as she sat back down. The woman still held in his arms whimpered.

"I was being polite, but now I'm going to give you a warning. This will be your only warning because you have decided to pull me into your vortex. If you do not stop this absurdity and walk away, there will be consequences. And I can assure you, that only one of us will be walking out of here today."

The man's mind suddenly shifted back to the panicked museum goers around him as the sound of police sirens screamed outside the building. His eyes flickered towards the windows, the innocent victims around the room crouched against walls and objects to try to avoid his waving gun.

His attention swung back to Natalya on the bench. "You! Come with me."

"I will do no such thing," she countered, continuing to stare at the sculpture in front of her, while in her coat pocket, her hand clutched a pen tightly.

The gun swung in front of her face. "I'll shoot."

195

Natalya calmly turned to face the gun. "Why would you bother doing that when you can just set your vest off and blow us all up? That's what you're really here to do, right? Do it. That is, unless you're scared."

As the man's eyes dropped, his mind trying to make sense of the conflicting emotions in his brain, Natalya quickly stood. One hand grabbed the man's extended wrist, pushing the gun up while she brought around her other hand, jabbing the metal tipped end into the soft flesh under his chin.

The gun exploded and screams erupted from innocent bystanders.

Detective Thomas had just opened his car door when the sound of gunfire echoed from within the museum. The police officers were on high alert as they continued to surround the building gathering information. Ducking behind vehicles he made his way closer to the frontlines.

"Sergeant, what's the situation?"

"Suicide bomber, but…"

A commotion burst from the front doors of the museum as scared civilians rushed out onto the evacuated plaza in front of the museum. Police officers carefully stepped forward to guide them safely away from the building.

"Victims say the suspect is dead," an officer blurted through Det. Thomas's ear piece, he shifted his attention back to the Sergeant.

"Send in the EDU."

A group of three men strapped into thick and heavy protective bomb gear slowly began to enter the building. After an agonizing fifteen minutes, they finally reported back the all clear for the site. Det.

Thomas found himself heading directly to the main security office to track down footage from the event.

The security manager pulled up the camera feeds showing the man enter the museum and snake his way through the rooms until finally taking a hostage inside the Rodin exhibit. His eyes immediately focused in on the curious, but familiar looking, visitor with short blonde hair sitting on a bench wearing a grey hat. The suspect approached her, the two appeared to be having a conversation.

"Is there any way we can get a better angle on her face?" he asked, pointing at the screen.

The security manager shook his head. "The only other view is from behind her."

He continued to watch the grainy footage showing the woman suddenly lunge at the man, blocking his gun as it went off, sending a bullet into the ceiling. The hostage clamored away screaming. The mysterious woman's free hand swung up towards the suspect's chin, his head knocking back. The suspect froze in place a moment before finally falling to the ground, the woman's head following it down as she watched him fall.

The mysterious woman knelt over him a moment, her hands doing something to the vest before she finally stood and walked away.

Det. Thomas pointed at the screen. "Where does she go?"

The camera facing the adjoining exhibit showed no signs of her entering as a rush of people ran through and fled the museum.

"Shit! Where did she go? What's between those rooms?"

"A door to the stairs."

"Can you get me footage from in there?"

The security manager shook his head. "Emergency exit, she most likely walked out the back."

Det. Thomas headed back down to the museum's main floor and towards the team still gathering evidence from the exhibit room, the suspect's body still flayed out on the floor. "Sergeant, what you got?"

Sergeant Lai turned to greet him. "Some of the hostages say that a woman attacked him."

"Security footage can confirm that, but I couldn't see what she did." The Sergeant knelt next to the body and pointed under the suspect's chin. Det. Thomas got down on the opposite side to observe the bloodied hole. "What caused that?"

The Sergeant looked up at him. "Can you believe a pen?"

"No shit."

"But not just any pen. This was a $1900 diamond point fountain pen, with black onyx cabochon and 18K gold. I had to Google that shit."

"Fancy."

"Yup. Perfect incision through the skull, penetrating the brain stem. I'd almost say that our mystery woman knew what she was doing."

"Let me know if you get anything from the pen."

"Will do." As Det. Thomas stood he glanced over at the large sculpture in front of the bench. "What the hell is that?"

Sergeant Lai stood and followed his gaze. "Exactly. The Gates of Hell."

"I'd say."

"No, that's what it's called, The Gates of Hell, by Rodin." Det. Thomas stepped closer, his eyes admiring the warped and confused dark figures writhing from the structure.

"Oh, one more thing for you Detective. Seems your mystery woman knows how to defuse a bomb. EDU says she happened to pull the wires connected to the trigger."

Det. Thomas turned back to the suspect lying on the floor. "Coincidence?"

Sergeant Lai shook his head. "Not a chance." He pulled open the suspects jacket to reveal the snaking wires woven throughout the vest. "Had she pulled any other wires it would have gone off."

The Axiom Cipher

(Book One of the Axiom Series)

Being a suspected terrorist was the least of Ana's problems when she finds herself on a ship destined to a slave labour camp in the Arctic. After being injected with an experimental virus which not only makes her immune to temperature, but increases her stamina, strength and healing capabilities; it also has the unfortunate effect of wreaking havoc with her hormones. All bets are off as the Axiom Virus fuses with her DNA, including her ability to resist the charms of an escaped convict named Keynes.

Secret military viruses, government conspiracies and world domination got nothing on Anastasia Grey. Now if only she could control her sexual appetite. But what can a girl do when she's got a virus coursing through her veins that feeds on death and sex?

Prologue

I don't remember when the last time was I saw my sister or anyone from my home town. After the great economic collapse of 2010, the world had changed. Countries began to crumble one after another as their corporate backbones gave out. Unable to sustain themselves they began looking beyond their borders for survival. Canada and the United States united with Mexico under the North American Union Act of 2015, but it was already too late. The Union could do little to stimulate the economy and people fell further into turmoil. People were jobless, starving, trying to do whatever they could to survive. Cities became commercial graveyards harbouring the underdogs of society. Theft, trade, murder and sex ran the streets.

Beyond the cities lay pockets of communities working hard to revert back to simpler times. Living off the lands, becoming one with nature again, and building better communities were their bible. The corporation had failed them, democracy, religion; all had left them now to fend for themselves. Unfortunately for me, man had been the one to fail me the most. The suffering man inflicts on himself is of the worst kind, worse than war or disease or money. It is the worst because no matter what destruction he has caused or pain he has inflicted on others, he still believes in hope. Behind every hope lays a truth.

I was born in a small community called Grovewood on an island off the West Coast. For those who survived the economic collapse and stuck through the political debacle of the North American Union Act, Grovewood was the ideal little community to pick up the pieces. However, becoming the ultimate stay-at-home mom, raising kids and tending the land while my husband brought home what food he could catch, wasn't my ideal life.

Across the Strait of Georgia sat the last great epicentre of the West Coast. Metro City was an amalgamation of the last remaining West Coast cities, of what had once been the District of Vancouver. It was a shithole – don't let anyone try to convince you otherwise. The streets buckled under the weather, nature and time. Once thriving office buildings now belonged to nature's best and man's worst. Drug addicts, criminals and thieves of the underworld ruled the streets. People abandoned all hope of survival for the countryside where the earth could grant them some vestige of a life.

What was left of the North American Union government wall holed up in the Midwest. Democracy was a dream as people scrambled for survival. It wasn't long before the military stepped in and began giving the orders. Their leader was a Stalinistic woman by the name of General Arrovian. Her first step to stabilize the economy was to round up all undesirables and place them in labour camps. Free labour meant that anything produced would yield a profit. Her primary course of action: to depose of all major cities' refuge and relegate them to the camps, thus clearing the way for economic amelioration. Democratic socialism at its worst.

The labour camps had been in commission for four years when I finally stepped foot in Metro City. I was twenty-five years old. It was 2029. My baby sister, Selina, made the trek with me. We settled nicely into a small harbour community called the Black Sholes. A small apartment over a pub gave us a roof over our heads and provided us with income as we served the best of the fishing and shipping clientele. Selina seemed to enjoy it and had even met some up-and-coming young businessman by the name of Autarky.

After work I took to the streets more and more, learning for myself how business was really conducted in Metro City. My lessons led me to a new problem, a man named Hahn. Little did I realize that he was only the beginning.

Chapter One – Metro City: Anastasia's Way

It sounded like the wood had cracked, splitting as it struck me across the shoulders. I fell to a knee, panting, my hair hanging in my face. "Is that the best you can do?" I picked myself up from the floor.

Hahn held the broken pieces of broomstick in his hands waiting for me to attack. "When will you ever learn, Ana?"

"Never." I lunged forward, feinting right. Twisting around, I brought my own broomstick down and whisked his feet out from under him.

The floor shook as he landed hard on his ass. "Touché," he croaked as I held the tip of my stick under his chin. "You've improved."

I grunted and walked away. Leaning my stick against the wall I grabbed my stainless steel flask of water and gulped it down, gasping for breath.

Hahn had been teaching me to fight ever since I hooked up with his gang of thieves in the spring. I liked to think of myself more as an entrepreneur – I did more than steal, I bartered business transactions. If someone needed something, I was their girl: pick up, transportation, investigation, whatever was needed I did – for a small fee of course.

We had been scoping out an abandoned hardware store for supplies when Hahn had decided it was the perfect opportunity to teach me how to think on my feet and use whatever was available to protect myself. I was a fast learner.

As Hahn stood up I dropped the flask and kicked it into the air. It deflected off his temple and ricocheted into a pile of debris. He lifted his hand to touch the cut above his right eye.

"Always be ready," I smirked.

"Ha ha," he replied sarcastically, wiping the blood from his hand onto his pants. "We better get going; the sun will be down soon."

I squinted, peering out the nearest window at the pink rays of setting sun as it slid behind the rise of office buildings along the horizon. Metro City wasn't the safest place to be poking around during the day, but at night anyone could be lurking in the shadows or perching in a stairwell; it could be a death trap if you didn't know where you were or how to defend yourself.

"You working tonight?" Hahn asked as he flung his bag of supplies over his shoulder.

"Nah, I gave my shift to Selina. She figures her new stalker is going to show up again."

"Stalker?"

"Yeah, some wannabe businessman who's got the hots for her. He shows up almost every night just to order drinks from her." I grabbed a bag of nails and threw it into my backpack before zipping it up and slinging it onto my back.

I watched as Hahn dug through a box looking for saw blades. His grey t-shirt stretched tight over sleek muscles. My eyes followed it down his narrow waist where it was tucked into his cargo pants. The muscles of his ass twitched with each movement. A well coifed goatee hung from his chin, his hair short and wavy. He was about ten years older than me, but like any man, never acted his age. "Think fast," he said, flinging one of the saw blades at my head.

I caught the blade in my hand, one of the tines puncturing the leather of my fingerless glove. Without thinking, I flung it back at him hitting his combat boot, lodging itself in the toe. "Jesus, shit!" he shouted, hopping up and down on his good foot. "I think you got my toe." He reached over and pulled the blade out, a red smear of blood spread out along the tines.

"Maybe one of these days you'll learn not to play with sharp objects."

He threw the blade down, grabbed a hand-held saw and headed out the door. With a smirk on my face, I followed him down the street.

We walked in silence for four blocks; apparently I had hurt his pride. "You know, I can take care of myself. I don't always need you looking over my shoulder or testing my reflexes."

With his brows furrowed he ignored me, shifting his bag across his back.

"I'm sorry, okay. I wasn't thinking. I just reacted. You're the one that—"

He stopped walking and I nearly bumped into him. "That's your problem, Ana. You don't think. You're stubborn and cocky and that could get you killed." He stormed off around the corner heading for the nearest SkyTrain terminal.

"Don't get you manties in a bunch," I mumbled.

Picking up the pace, I passed him and began jogging up the terminal stairs towards the main platform. Without waiting, I jumped down onto the track which led out across the city. As Hahn caught up I adjusted my ponytail and gazed out over the city's horizon. Office buildings and shopping centres dotted the cityscape. Smoke rose into the air from sporadic locations: shelters, bonfires, garbage and drug dens. A cool breeze picked up blowing in from the ocean, bringing with it the scent of sea salt. I shivered, standing there in my tank top and torn jeans.

Over the years I've watched summer turn into representations of fall – and I'm not talking about the changing of the seasons. When I was a kid the Global Climatology Association had declared a global warming epidemic. Man-made carbon dioxide emissions were wreaking havoc on our environment, melting ice caps, raising sea levels and killing polar bears. They were wrong. Shorter hotter summers and longer colder winters soon had the scientific community lodged in a constant debate of ecological proportions. The discovery of temperature data altered by the GCA scientists in order to produce figures supporting their man-made theory of destruction only led to further the political agenda of the global elite. Global warming, global cooling; it didn't matter to them what was happening so long as they were able to continue their tyrannical quest of suppressing people's rights.

The SkyTrain hadn't been in operation in years; it was a glorified highway of the sky. Most of the useable railcars had been converted into luxury drug dens. Regardless, the track was the safest way to travel on foot. By keeping above the streets it was easier to watch out for any trouble that lurked nearby. The winding tracks made the city more accessible, gas was hard to come by and expensive. Most vehicles sat like tombs along the streets, a reminder of just how far we'd strayed from dreams of a better future. One thing we were lucky to have in Metro City, electricity. Our city was powered by hydroelectricity, so unless the rivers dried up, we were still able to remain out of the dark ages. Naturally the military had taken control over the hydro plants as part of their plan to build a better future, regulating usage. For now, the service was free; it was a privilege, their "free" labour providing the upkeep of services.

Radio broadcasts, emitted with permission from the local army commander, kept the populace updated on all current events. Generally, they used it to hark off propaganda for a new social order. Help rebuild our communities for a better tomorrow type of crap. It was easy to brainwash smaller communities; they even had some of them establish farm collectives to manage and grow produce. Everyone who participated reaped in the benefits of fresh fruit, vegetables and dairy. Any excess was brought into the cities or other communities where it could be traded for other goods. Some people still chose to eat from the ocean, but if you were smart you stayed away from that hot nuclear mess, nothing but a slush pool from nuclear disasters across the Pacific. Sometimes the starving can't afford to be picky.

Hahn smacked me hard on the shoulder as he walked past, heading out of the terminal and onto the main concourse of track. We began our trek over the city streets, nearing the ocean. On one side, an abandoned bus and rail terminal which had been converted into a make-shift military command centre, on the other, the domed remnants of a science centre. The bulbs were all broken or burnt out on the centre's gulf ball exterior, leaving it looking like an abandoned futuristic house. Continuing, the track twisted back into the city, past a large shopping centre, before finally heading into a residential district. The track led towards the Fraser River that emptied into the Strait. Following the curve of the river inland we made our way to Twenty-Second Street station.

As we climbed onto the main platform I could hear heavy panting. "What's the matter old man? Having trouble keeping up?"

"What?"

Once on the platform, the panting turned into growls. Slowly I looked up trying to locate the noise. A few metres away, a brindle coloured pit bull had positioned itself between us and the exit stairs. Its lips were pulled back baring its teeth, drool and foam dripped onto the floor as it snarled.

Chapter Two – Metro City: Keynesian Economics

I breathed in the crisp aroma of the first cup of steaming coffee I'd had in years. This made my freedom taste even sweeter. Bitter sweet. Years in the military eating MREs was enough to give anyone gut-rot. Now if it was pre-packaged, I didn't want it.

Metro City was not what I expected. It was a rat hole, straight up. Vagrants, thieves, prostitution, corruption – you name it, this city was crawling with it. Not that I cared much. I'd just spent the last few years behind a chain link fence in the Arctic. My goal, get as far South as possible before anyone notices I'm gone. The last guy who went AWOL was found a week later frozen in the ice, but I was a lot smarter than him.

Thanks to a small vial of an experimental virus, I was the closest thing to military-grade genetic perfection. And, I was free.

The old man behind the counter kept screwing with the radio antenna playing static garble. His wife was a little too eager to please by the way she kept checking on me. Bet they could remember the good ol' days before anyone had even heard of the New World Agenda and all its conspiracies. Shit. I'd give anything for just being able to buy a potato without having to pay a damn Carbon Tax.

Carbon Tax. Whoever thought that shit up should be shot. The Government tried to pass it off as a solution to the impending fate of Global Warming. That was a joke. Instead, we ended up with a new Ice Age which now covered half of what used to be Canada. I'd like to say thank god capitalism is dead, but the morons who caused the world economy to collapse are still in power. And they will still suck whatever they can out of you.

A female voice erupted from the static of the radio. "As the North American Union government continues to amend the Union Act of 2015, General Arrovian continues her quest to establish economic development in local communities in the hopes of stabilizing the economy. A representative of the General confirmed yesterday that the labour camps, established five years ago promoting free labour of undesirables and criminals, have been steadily increasing. General Arrovian assures all citizens of the Union that economic stability is within our grasp..."

Fucking propaganda.

I bolted from the café and onto the street. Military convoys were patrolling the streets. I ducked into the nearest alley, my shoulder thudding against a large garbage can as I braced myself and watched them pass.

Undesirables and criminals my ass. I've seen what they've been taking from the streets to the labour camps. And it sure as hell wasn't undesirables and criminals – at least, not all of them. The country was their corporation and they had a quota to meet. Any. Way. They. Could.

I turned around and headed down the alley. A sign reading *Interior Solutions* screamed at me from the hardware store across the street at the end of the alley. "Interior Solutions" was what we used to call the method of punishment we dealt out in the labour camps. One, because it was "in" the camp. Two, because it was our "solution" to the problems with delinquent prisoners. And three, because no one on the outside knew we did it.

The stagnant smell of sea water stung my nostrils. I hated the ocean. This city was the last greatest port along the West Coast. Earthquakes had ravaged Los Angeles years ago leaving it looking more like a war zone. An uninhabitable wasteland.

I dashed across the street towards the old railway station. Right on the harbour was the dilapidated remains of a giant spherical building which looked more like a monstrous golf ball. A faded sign read: *Sc n e W rl*. Whatever futuristic anomalies it used to hold were nothing but a joke whose punch line was long since forgotten.

Follow the train tracks and get the fuck out of here were the plan. The only problem, the station was being used as a military base of operations – and I needed a map of all available train routes. Trekking from Alaska to here was nothing; it was near void of any human populace, so following the coastline or the transport highway was easy. The further south, the more people. More people meant more military influence. Which meant a greater chance of the Keynes-man getting caught.

A mini drone whizzed over my head. Shit.

I bolted for an old auto body yard where three undesirables stood huddled around a barrel with fire spurting out the top.

"We were here first buddy!" one of them yelled after me.

"Well, you won't be here for long," I replied as I heard a commanding voice boom from the bull horn of a Humvee which was now hot on my tail.

"Stop vagrant!" the bull horn blasted. Did they really think that shit worked? Who would be stupid enough to stop?

I turned around just in time to see the vehicle pull into the yard where the squatters stood with their hands in the air waiting for their fate to come take them away. I guess people really were that stupid.

Wheels squealed in the distance behind me. I threw myself over a chain link fence and into an alley. More wheels squealed. Bursting from the alley I ran smack into the hood of a black Humvee.

Turning to flee, my chest jabbed into the business end of an M249 Light Machine Gun.

"Hey guys," I jeered. "Nice night for a run."

There was a small click as I felt something lodge itself in my back. A jolt of energy tore through my body, frying every nerve. My knees shook uncontrollably and I collapsed on the ground twitching.

"Th…that w…wasn't very nice," I managed to spit out through clenched jaw before the butt of a rifle came down on my head.

When I came to, I was kneeling and chained to the floor of a Prisoner Transport Vehicle with my three new friends. The truck bumped along. A small light glowed from the roof casting ghoulish shadows across the men's faces. Their heads hung like they had already welcomed their fate.

I wasn't so eager.

This sucked. Guess I was a little out of touch with the world; I was getting sloppy. Next time I'd make sure to pay more attention.

The vehicle finally came to a stop. Doors slammed as men exited the cab. More doors. There were other vehicles outside. Muffled voices. And then everything was quiet.

The air was humid and thick inside our cramped compartment. Small noises of the vehicle cooling and settling broke the silence as we waited. What *were* we waiting for?

Finally the latch ground on the door and it swung open. It was night. Two men held the arms of a petite young female. She was quiet. Her shoulder length hair hung in her face as they shoved her inside. The door slammed shut.

My balls grew tight. If I hadn't been chained to the floor I'd have done her right then – audience and all. Hell, the thought of those three weasels watching made my nuts throb more. She had a fine little hard body. Toned. Her skin was probably silky smooth. It had been too long since I had a good fuck.

Kill something or fuck something. Maybe fuck her then kill the three amigos over there. Then fuck her again. That sounded like a plan.

Goddamn virus. All it ever made me want to do was kill or fuck something. Not like I was complaining, but when you couldn't do either one of those it left you with a serious case of the jitters.

The virus had been developed by a man named Friedman Bilderberg, a nutty little man with glasses too big for his face. Long white strands of hair draped across his balding head. He was short and frail looking.

Axiom Pharmaceuticals was his brainchild. Never make a deal with devil, so they say. Someone should have told Bilderberg that when he decided to accept a contract with the United States military years ago. He was still young, in his thirties when they hired him to develop a virus for soldiers in the Middle East. Something that wouldn't make them so vulnerable to heat and dehydration. Something more Combat Effective.

Was it all part of the New World Agenda? Who really knows?

The project evolved, as did everything the military did.

I was fresh out of boot camp when I was stationed at Axiom Pharmaceuticals in Miles City, Montana – the last place in the world you'd expect to find a bio-hazard lab developing viral weapons. I became the man's Over-trained Babysitter – OBS I called it. Needless to say, I was bored shitless.

Mix and mingle with the civilian population always left me bruised and battered with a hangover waking up in the brig. I was a regular brig rat. My home away from home. Anything was better than standing inside those sterile white washed halls smelling disinfectant all day.

The defecation hit the oscillation during the Economic Collapse in 2010. The grounds around the lab were turned into military central. After the North American Union Act, my babysitting job turned into managing a house of horrors.

General Arrovian had sanctioned the use of human subjects for all of Bilderberg's work. They were supposed to be volunteers. I later found out that the first round of "volunteers" were actually prison inmates. All of them died.

New "volunteers" were brought in. An entire housing complex had to be built to accommodate them. We're not talking five star hotel either. Not even one star. The rooms had been designed to mimic environmental stresses on the subjects. Torture chambers to test the effectiveness of the virus.

As the virus evolved, so did my role.

My reputation as a brig rat gave my superiors something to latch on to when my behaviour became too unpredictable. Some of the test subjects were ready for stage two of the trials: physical stimulation. Finally, I thought I was going to be able to put a little of my combat effectiveness training to use, until a manual with the title *KUBARK Counterintelligence Interrogation* was placed in my hands.

Everyone was a suspected terrorist. The General was even offering the populace payment for any information leading to an arrest of a suspected terrorist. Needless to say, if you hated your neighbour, he became a suspected terrorist. And he ended up in one of my rooms.

First, I'd fuck with their heads.

"Name?"

"Joseph Finley."

That was too easy. "Joseph. Joseph, it says here that you are being accused of terrorist activities."

"That's not true. I love my country. I'm innocent."

"Well, Joseph. If you were innocent, then you wouldn't be talking to me. Would you?"

First, I'd splay out a variety of bright shiny tools with sharp pointy edges. The microscopic changes on their faces as they began to realize their predicament always sent a rush of adrenaline through me.

"You don't want me to have to hurt you, do you Joseph? Because I'm gonna have to hurt you if you don't cooperate."

This was where the pleas and begging began. Hardly worth my time.

"I'll tell you what, Joseph. Let's start small." Gently, I'd pick up the syringe carrying the virus and hold it delicately in my hand.

"What's that?"

"Oh this?" I'd look at it innocently. "This will become your new best friend." Then I'd jab the needle into their arm violently just so they'd remember what real pain used to feel like before I unleashed my arsenal.

I was good at what I did. The best. But I was beginning to enjoy the violence – torture – and death. They always screamed like Satan was upon them as I stood with my blow torch ready to begin. Blood curdling screams as I began. And then silence when they realized that they couldn't feel a damn thing. That kinda took the initial fun out of it.

As time went on they'd begin to whimper. Begging me to just put them out of their misery. Seeing torture you couldn't feel, especially done to you, could be just as traumatizing as the anticipation of painful torture. And there was nothing they could do.

217

That would fuck with anyone's head. Especially mine.

Once the system of labour camps was set up within the Union I put in for a transfer. The Bering Glacier in the Arctic wasn't my first choice, but it wasn't Axiom Pharmaceuticals.

Above ground it looked like any normal military base, with the exception of a small laboratory. I didn't know what they were producing, and I didn't want to. My job was supposed to be to assist in the transport of labourers.

Where they were hiding these labourers was another question. The base hadn't been built to accommodate any civilians – I assumed the labour camp was somewhere on the ice flow. Trucks started arriving and unloading people. They'd file into the Main Camp Administration Offices and then I'd never see them again.

"Keynes, right?" Captain Habakkuk asked as he passed me one day.

"Yes, sir!" I was a real keener.

"You transferred in from Miles City, right?"

"Yes, sir."

"I've got a new assignment I think you'd be perfect for."

Chapter Three – Moscow: The Priest and The Marshal

I watched Anatoly raise the gun, point it to the man's temple. He was young, Anatoly. But he was a good boy.

Music from Club Corbie thumped behind us across the parking lot. White flakes of snow drifted from grey clouds spreading a light dust over our shoulders.

I watched Anatoly's face. His jaw grew tight, his eyes narrowed. Adrenaline pumped through his veins. The man kneeling before him sniffled, whimpering. Once he pulled that trigger there would be no going back. This was his requiem.

He squeezed the trigger. A shot rang out as the bullet entered the man's head, fragments of skull, brains and blood burst from the other side. The body shuddered, curled over and fell to the ground.

I was fifteen. Fifteen years old when a man tried to rob me in the back alley behind Filippov Bakery on Tverskaya Street.

My father gave me a soviet NR-40 nozh razvedchika – a scout's knife – for my fifteenth birthday. "You are a man now, a Vory," he had said.

And yes, now I was a man. Standing over the dead body of another man, blood pouring from his neck onto the street. My hands were covered in the thick, sticky, red liquid. I wiped the blade of the knife on my pant-leg and shoved it back into the waist of my pants. The metal was cold against my skin.

I stepped from the shadows of the alley and onto the street. My knees grew weak and I collapsed, puking. On the back of my sleeve, I wiped the acidy liquid from my mouth.

My feet felt large and clumsy as I stumbled down the street. The reflection I saw in the fish market window was not my own. The creature was rabid, a haggard sea monster which had risen from the shallows in search of…

Death?

"Boy, are you alright?" I heard someone say.

As I looked up, I heard them gasp.

Blood streaked down my face and dripped from my sandy brown hair. Bloodshot eyes strained to understand the look of horror on the man's face as he pulled out his phone and punched at the numbers.

I drifted by.

Time ceased and the world slowed. Things no longer held meaning. Images blurred. Tears.

"Boy!"

My feet shuffled to a stop.

"Boy!"

I grew faint as I tilted my head towards the voice. A dark figure loomed over me. Strong hands grabbed my shoulders and led me to the backseat of a car. Streets blurred as I sat on the cool, smooth seat. Stale smoke infused everything.

I blinked.

When I opened my eyes I was sitting on a metal chair in a small room. The green paint was chipped on the matching grey metal table in front of me.

"Did you do it, boy?" a deep, booming voice asked.

Do what? I thought. *Kill that man? Yes.*

"Why did you do it, boy?"

Why? I wanted to live.

In prison they threw me into a cell with forty other men. Men! There were only ten beds. It wreaked of sweat, urine, feces, cigarettes…death.

The men were thin. Bones protruded from their ribs and shoulders. Ink stained their leather skin.

They were beautiful.

Gods of war. These were the warriors that protected us in our sleep. These were the men who made love to you with words during the day and then slit your throat at night. These were the Kings of the Underworld.

And I thought they were beautiful.

Their bodies were adorned with God's symbols. Symbols of oppression. Symbols of loss, of love. Honesty. They bore the pain of us all and wore it proudly like a suit of armour telling us their story.

They were my family now. These men. Under their watchful eyes I too grew to be a man.

"Vory," Pascal said to me one day. "Sometimes as a man, we must endure hardship so that those we love may live free. Do you love your country?"

"Yes."

"Remember. She is yours. She will provide you with everything you need to survive. No one can take her away from you."

I nodded, trying to understand. He threw his skinny arm around my shoulders. The ink of a bloody cross, fresh, on the back of his hand dangled in my face.

"We are in hell, but we are safe. Outside is our kingdom. In here, we suffer for the sins of the world. Out there," he pointed to the glow of light seeping through our tiny window, "it is our job to uphold the justice of the streets. To free the people from their hell. To absolve their sins."

Life now had purpose. I was no longer a murderer. I was a man freeing people of the injustices of the world. I was their King. Their God. I would not fail them.

I was released from prison when I was eighteen. Was it because I was a minor when I entered? Because I had paid my dues? Or was it because they no longer had room in their cramped abyss and I had won their lottery? The Freedom Lottery we called it. There was no rhyme or reason; it was as if they just got tired of seeing your ugly face. I could have killed fifty men, it wouldn't have mattered.

Thoughts of my family flooded my mind. My parents. My little sister, Malina. Did they miss me? Did they know where I had been? What had happened? Russia's antiquated justice system left much to be desired. Children ran away from home every day; it was none of their business what became of them. I was a statistic. A number.

Our small apartment in the Federal District sat quiet. I stood watching for an hour from the street before I could will my feet to the front step. My hand slid along the rusty iron banister. My boots scraped against the rocks and leaves on the short steps.

The door looked so small. Smaller than I remembered. I squeezed my hand into a fist. Cold fingers pressed against my palm as I lifted it.

The door swung open. A short woman with golden greying hair and dull blue eyes stared at me. Stood silently. Waiting. The muscles on her face twitched, first surprise, sadness, anger and then relief. Then…

"Vory!" She took me into her arms, her rough dry hands squeezing and rubbing. "You are back!" She held me away. "You are so thin."

"I was…" I wanted to tell her where I had been, but I didn't want to take her happiness away. It was selfish of me.

"You have to leave," she spat hurriedly. "Your father will be home soon, he can't see you."

"What?"

"How could you shame this family, Vory? How could you be so selfish? Now go."

My face stung as if I had been slapped. My chest ached as if I were shot. My stomach turned as if I had been punched.

The door slammed shut.

Leaves skittered across the cement. Branches clicked and creaked. Grey clouds hung low, so low they nearly touched the golden domes of the Elokhovo Cathedral, its crosses reaching to the heavens. A raven gronked from the naked branch of a tree. I watched as it took to the air flying high over the cathedral landing next to its companions on the bell tower.

A tear gathered in the corner of my eye and then rolled down my cheek, catching in the whiskers on my face and getting lost in their wake. And as I looked up at the luminous crosses sitting atop the great shiny golden domes I remembered what Pascal had told me.

This is my kingdom. These are my people and I am their god. I decide who lives or dies. I take no gratification in their happiness or suffering. These streets are my destiny. My sanctuary. I was their Priest. I was their Marshal. I was the law.

The men behind those prison walls were my brothers. My family. From these tears I would rise up to be born again.

Now, thirteen years later I stand on this hill, I overlook the city. My city. My Moskva. Lights shimmer and dance in the night. Music booms from the club behind me. Blood drains into the dirt.

The Gospel of Amare

How do you defeat terrorism when politics, war, religion, and science fail?

Amare was convinced she had the answer and she was willing to risk her life to prove it.

I never set out to become a super hero, only to graduate with a degree in Philosophy. I was in the middle of writing my final thesis when the Revolution broke out. A ground-breaking thesis I thought. One that had the potential to alter the course of human history. Little did I know that my theory was about to turn into a live subject testing ground with me as the guinea pig.

AMARE

I never set out to become a super hero, only to graduate with a degree in Philosophy. I was in the middle of writing my final thesis when the Revolution broke out. A ground-breaking thesis I thought. One that had the potential to alter the course of human history. Little did I know that my theory was about to turn into a live subject testing ground with me as the guinea pig.

The fascinating thing about philosophy is that it's more than just opinions based on theoretical religious interpretations of ancient cultural references. There's so many hidden meanings that you need to become a little bit of a treasure hunter in linguistic antiquities in order to decipher the allusions from the illusions to produce the gospel of the universe.

I don't want to bore you with technical lingo, so perhaps I should dive in to the part about becoming a super hero.

From ancient religious texts to ancient philosophers, to the Enuma Elish, I was enthralled with the vibrant stories about the world that once was. A student of philosophy is of no use if they do not understand the history from whence it came. My thirst for knowledge always left me home alone on a Saturday night while everyone else partook in the cultural tradition of the young adult – the night club.

I had studied the finer points of ancient philosophical musings and had decided to write my thesis on an analogy of philosophical treatise in the modern age. What I found most fascinating was that it didn't matter if I sourced a religious text, the occult, science, new age, or standard philosophy, they all held true to a basic core principle – a universal axiom.

This axiom was so self-evident that proving it – the complete opposite of an axiom – was going to be more of a challenge. However,

226

I was determined to prove myself worthy of this knowledge and accept it as a belief. In essence, it goes like this: the universe is made up of energy. Everything is energy. Our perception of this energy through the element of light, mixed with personal beliefs, alters this energy to produce the hologram we believe to be our reality.

Still with me?

Underlying this belief of our reflected reality is a basic algebraic principle – all equations must balance. The left side of the equation must equal the right side.

The web of deceit and lies, rhetoric and hate from the Commonwealth Party spread like a virus across the country. The only thing I thought they had in common, was their wealth. Their nationalistic socialism went beyond preserving our borders from refugees, quickly turning into totalitarian existentialism. Fear and hate propaganda became their weapon of choice. It was their rhetoric that prompted me to awaken from my pre-programmed sleep. Finally, I understood how to cure the plague that poisoned our world.

Love.

I could hardly believe that it was something so simple, but I was willing to bet my life to prove it.

As I walked along the seawall downtown an alert came up on my phone informing me that a handful of gunmen had just entered the mall in my area and to remain calm and get off the streets. I would remain calm alright, but I had a better idea. I was going to test my theory. I was not only taking back my rights, I was taking back my power from those who terrorized the country. I was invoking my universal sovereignty.

People ran screaming hysterically past me. Shots rang out in the distance. I remained true to my course, focused, calm, and filled with the all-knowing truth that I alone was the sole creator of my reality. And within my reality, love was the only cure for its current plague.

My body floated through the doors as if they didn't exist. My senses heightened, observing the chaos around me as nothing more than a mirage. In my mind, I knew what I wanted. I could see it in all its glory. This was my temple, this was my soul, and these people were a part of me. We were all connected, and together we were more powerful than any terrorist with a gun.

Bodies lay in pools of blood along the main concourse. Chairs, benches and potted trees were strewn about as if a tornado had whipped through. Shouts echoed from the central clock tower in the centre of the mall. Ahead, I could just make out a small group of people huddled together, covered in blood. A man with a machine gun shot at someone as he stood before his victims.

My feet came to a stop. Glancing to my right was a kitchenware store. Behind the counter, a vast array of very large kitchen and hunting knives. I perused the selection, picking out my top five sturdy choices, slipping them into the waist of my skinny jeans before heading back out to the hall.

Their fearless leader – an ironic term considering he was anything but fearless – stood like a giant atop a bench shouting at his hostages. My fingers caressed the leather handle of the knife as I steadied myself, raised my arm into the air and let loose the dagger. I flew into a full run after it as it lodged itself into the man's back. He fell to the floor, the gun slid to the side as he tried unsuccessfully to grab the knife now stuck in his kidneys.

Sliding into home plate, I snatched up the gun and jumped to my feet. Sweat poured from the man's face, crumpled in pain, his brows furrowed, narrowing with hate as he looked up to find me at the trigger end of his gun, the nose pointed at his chest.

"I forgive you," was all I could utter before I pulled the trigger. His chest exploded as his body flew back against the pale tile floor now adorned in blood.

The shoppers screamed in horror.

Another armed man running at full tilt sprang from around the corner, his gun held upright. Without thinking, I aimed, and as he came to a stop my finger squeezed the trigger, sending him flying against the wall.

Outside, I could hear sirens. Unfazed, I continued through the mall, stalking the terrorists.

In my heart was only the warm swell of love for these men so full of hate and fear. I was not exacting revenge, I was cleansing the air. These acts needed to come to a clean ending; if I allowed the police or military to intervene they would only continue to feed the fear and hate, perpetuating the cycle. Adding to the negative equation. I needed to swing the balance of that equation in the other direction.

A shot rang out past my head causing a tile on the wall to explode. I turned to the left just in time to see the man take aim again from between two large ferns.

I inhaled slowly. This was my reality. This man was afraid. The universe would protect me. The universe would guide me through this safely. Quickly I pulled a knife from my waist and flung it towards the man; it struck deep into his thigh. The moment he grabbed at it I raised my gun and took a shot. As I lowered the gun, he fell to the floor.

More screams erupted from within a large sporting goods store. Shots were fired amongst the shouting. I continued with a steady pace, the heels of my boots clicking down the hall as I neared the store. A man stood on the checkout counter dressed in black, his face partially covered with a black scarf. I stopped at the entrance as we stared at one another.

He pointed his gun at me. "You! Let the power of the Almighty rain down on your kind! May your blood spill into the earth and your children be sacrificed in the name of democracy!"

Without hesitation I tilted my gun up and pulled the trigger. The man fell to the counter, his body spilling onto the floor as his hostages screamed in terror.

"I am the Almighty. That is my democracy," I replied under my breath.

I dropped the gun and continued walking out the far exit of the store as the anti-terror units stormed the mall looking for a fight. They were too late.

Back in my apartment, I plopped myself down on the couch with a sigh. All in a day's work it seemed. I could hardly believe it worked. I didn't even have a scratch, a bruise, nothing. And I had stared death in the face four times! With love in my heart and the universe on my side, I had successfully used the fundamental philosophical principle of my belief in the power of love to overcome hate and fear.

Over the next few days my super hero persona took on a life of its own in the media thanks in part to the survivors at the mall that day. And as luck would have it, my identity remained hidden due to the fact that the terrorists had dismantled all the security cameras at the mall. At least, until a blurry thirty second clip appeared on the internet, shot from one of the hostage's cellphones.

"Reports are surfacing from survivors of the Harbour City Mall terrorist take-over of an unknown vigilante who saved them. Reportedly, the vigilante was a young female who bravely walked the mall wielding knives at the terrorists and killing them. Remarkably, reports conclude that she later just, walked out of the mall and disappeared into the streets."

And so I had found myself with a new career. Unfortunately, the title of "vigilante" left a small knot in my stomach. My intent was not vengeance. My intent was purely of a more divine nature. Had I just justified my actions in the same manner of the terrorists?

Now, not only was I a vigilante, I was also a terrorist…with a very philosophical and moral dilemma. Do I continue to use my knowledge for good even if in the process others must die? Or, do I let the universe play out the course of events, even if it means that innocent people must die?

It was a no brainer.

I had to continue to intervene, not only for the good of my own conscience, but in order to give the people something to believe in. Somehow, I needed to use my knowledge to show the world that we didn't need to fall victim to chaos, fear and hate. That if we chose differently, it would affect the outcome of our reality. That with just a thought, we could change the world.

My first course of action, to change the perception of my actions from those of a vigilante, to those of a saint. I needed to let the people know that my actions were not out of malice, but full of virtue and benevolence. A modern day Joan of Arc, without all the visions. Crossed with the devotion of Mother Teresa, without all the praying.

As the sun rose on the horizon I walked down to the church square in the centre of town. The great Cathedral of the All Saints sat solid and firm, holding its formidable and impressive stone gaze towards the large parliament complex opposite it. Throughout history it was a constant reminder to the people that our own laws are not above those of God. This belief was truer than they realized.

The morning rays of sun glinted off the golden cross on its perch. In cliché fashion, a dove fluttered across the roof and disappeared into the sky. I sat on a nearby bench and watched the colours of the cathedral change and shift with the light. I was aware of someone sitting down beside me, but remained transfixed in my gaze.

"In times like this, it's comforting to know that God is always with us," a soothing, gravely, male voice spoke with a hint of Scottish accent. I nearly swooned.

"It is. It's a shame people don't understand."

"Many have lost their faith."

"They have, but sometimes it takes a great tragedy for them to find it again."

"Yes, but it is never too late."

"No." I glanced out of the corner of my eye, taking note of the older gentleman next to me dressed head to toe in black with a small square of white at his neck. He was naturally handsome with thick dark hair, piercing blue eyes, and a strong nose. He was tall and fit. I politely smiled as our eyes met.

"You seem troubled. No doubt the events of yesterday have caused you great concern."

"They have," I replied.

"I hope I have been able to comfort you in some way."

"You have." I gave a small smile. Something about this priest stirred something in my chest. Something I had never felt before. I have never been a religious person, but I have always been curious.

232

"I am just on my way to mass if you'd like to join me?" We locked eyes and I could see there was a confidence and knowing which emanated from his soul, as if he too believed without doubt in the power of something greater.

I followed him into the vaulted hall of the cathedral. Elaborate murals and gold leafing brought an elegance to its simple design, wrapping a warmth around the hazel pews which sat in neat rows. I slid into the front row, a few terrified souls trickled in amongst the hall.

He stepped up on the dais and turned to face the congregation. "Let us pause and reflect in memory of those who lost their lives yesterday," he began. I couldn't help but remain transfixed on his facial expressions as he spoke, muting out everything he said until the final, "Amen."

My eyes snapped back to reality as he sat down beside me. "My name is Gabriel." He offered his hand.

"Amare."

"That's quite the name to live up to."

"As is yours."

"God is my strength. I'd like to think I'm doing pretty well." He chuckled softly.

"So do I." Our eyes met and a warm burst of energy erupted within my chest. "Father-."

"Gabriel."

"Gabriel … how does someone become a Saint?"

He leaned back in the pew. "Well, it can happen many ways. First, a person must live a faithful and pure life of love in the eyes of God. There is no *one* way; it's a subjective procedure based purely on ideologies. Then, you have to die." He glanced over at me.

"I have to die?"

There was something about the way he raised his eyebrow that sent a tingling sensation through my arm next to him. "And then after the person dies, They, the Church, must wait a minimum of five years. After that there is an investigation to determine if the person lived their life with sufficient holiness. From the investigation, the Congregation must show proof of heroic virtue, there must be verified miracles attributed to prayers made to the individual. After, They, the candidate, are canonised, there must be more prayers and miracles and then finally the pope may declare them a Saint."

"So no one alive has ever become a Saint?"

"No."

"Interesting." I leaned back as he leaned forward.

"Why do you ask?"

"Oh you know, I was just thinking about the terrorist attack at the mall yesterday. They're calling the person who saved the hostages a vigilante. But I thought that maybe that person wasn't doing it out of revenge. Maybe they killed those terrorists out of virtue."

Gabriel inhaled and sat up straighter. "I would have to agree with you."

"You would?"

"Absolutely. God works in mysterious ways, and saving lives definitely falls under acts of virtue. However, a true Saint never seeks the approval of their virtues, they merely serve for the greater good."

Well, I certainly wasn't seeking approval. But he was right, it was my ego which was bruised by the label of vigilante. "Thank you Fa-, I mean, Gabriel. You have been very insightful." We stood, shook hands, and I left. I couldn't resist turning back one last time to look at him as I walked out, only to find that he hadn't moved and continued to stare at me. A ray of sunlight from an overhead window streamed through, bathing him in its essence. I chuckled under my breath at the odds of that happening.

Remember Me

(Book 1: The Descendants of Poseidia)

Ajax is over 5,000 years old. A survivor of the ancient civilization of Poseidia which once thrived amongst the Atlas Mountains in the Sahara Desert. Gifted with the knowledge of his ancient masters, he pledged his life to guard the history and knowledge of his people until humanity ceased to exist.

Forced to marry a princess of his ancient homeland before it was violently destroyed, only to have the first King of Egypt kill her before his eyes, he vowed to never stop waiting and searching for her soul to return to him.

Adopted as a child, Renee had never known where she came from. But her entire life has been consumed with trying to uncover an ancient past she wasn't even sure ever existed.

Then one day from across a crowded café she sees him, the man of her dreams. Tall, dark and handsome in every sense, with the most vibrant pale green eyes she's unable to look away from. All she knows is that she's in love with him.

Soon her reality is turned upside down as she learns that she's not quite who she thinks she is.

Prologue

Egypt – 3266 BC – King's Temple of Neith

Immense fires burned in the cauldrons placed throughout the great hall of the temple. Pillars of stone rose to the heavens, carved and painted with prayers and rituals to the Egyptian Goddess Neith, the bringer of creation. Shadows danced on the walls as a cool breeze swept in from the Nile delta. My sandals slapped against the stone as I made my way across the hall towards the entrance overlooking the river. The stars shone brightly in the night sky.

My thoughts drifted to my homeland in the west. The great land of Poseidia now laid strife with warring amongst the brothers of Belial. And here I stand, patiently awaiting their own destruction, a priest of the Law of One, noble disciple of High Priest Sonchis, sent as emissary of our lands during the great exodus to spread the word of the Law of One in order to bring peace and knowledge to the distant lands before the sons of Belial cast out their deceptions.

A commotion came from beyond the temple walls, Ax-Tell burst through the front gate. He searched the yard and upon spotting me, ran in my direction shouting. "He knows! He knows!" He sprinted up the stairs and landed at my feet. "The King, he knows."

"He knows about what?"

"Assen-ni. He knows about her. He's on his way now with his guard. Where is she?"

"She is in the bath house."

"Quickly, you must get her out of here before they arrive. I'll have the horses brought around back. Head for Gipuzkoa. I'll send word to Sonchis and then follow as soon as I can."

I made my way through the darkened stairwell. I could feel the warmth of the bath house rising up to caress my face and stifle my breath. A scream echoed against the stone walls spurring me faster as I flew into the main bath chamber to find Assen-ni in the clutches of an armed soldier.

"You are in the Temple of Neith of the great King Narmer. Why have you desecrated her holy priestess?"

"I would ask you the same thing." From the shadows stepped forward King Narmer, the light from the wavering torches along the walls reflecting off the gold of his headdress. The wings of his golden chest plate seeming to flutter with the flames. He took a step towards Assen-ni. "Imagine my surprise when I discovered that one of my most holy of priestesses had betrayed her King and her vows to Neith."

The solder held her fast, her eyes locked hard with mine, pleading for help. I could sense her fear reaching out to my heart. "You're Highness must be mistaken. I can assure you that Assen-ni has kept her faith devoutly as a priestess of the Law of One to your holy land."

"Has she?" The King reached forward and tore at the thin cloth covering her body, revealing the small bump protruding from her stomach. "I demand to know how such a faithful servant has found herself with child. Immaculate conception by your God perhaps?" Slowly his head turned to face me, his eyes narrowing. "Or, perhaps by a priest in this temple?"

"Great Lord of the two Lands, my humble apologies. We will find this traitor and make sure that he is dealt with accordingly."

Narmer reached to his side and pulled a small blade, the fire light gleamed off the polished surface. "Be sure that you do." In one swift movement he inserted the blade into her belly and sliced to the side, spilling blood onto the floor at her feet. Her face contorted with shock, seemingly wanting to scream but unable to allow the sound to escape. Her hands shook as she tried helplessly to hold her abdomen. His hand gently caressed her face. "Now sweet priestess, I send you back to your maker where you can beg his forgiveness for your sins." Slowly the blade of the knife slid into her chest, piercing her heart. He gently pulled it out, wiping the blood off on her dress before storing it at his side.

My world seemed to slow and dull. There was movement around me and a dim reflection of voices, but all I could see was Assen-ni drifting to the floor as a feather plucked from a wing. Somehow I was at her side, holding her to my chest, my face pressed against hers. Her breath was shallow and filled with blood. I pressed my forehead to hers, looking deep into her eyes as I whispered my last prayer to her. "Our love burns through eternity and its fire will never be extinguished, for it is the Law of One and we are the children of Poseidia. My soul will search for you and bring you home. Remember me."

About The Author

Kimberly O'Neill as over a dozen books on Amazon. This author has a degree in Creative Writing and History and is a self-labeled polymath/autodidact. Nothing is too out of her realm of learning, especially if it'll make a great story. She loves travel and photography and is a hardcore romantic somewhere deep down in her cold dark heart. You can also find a collection of erotic and romance on Amazon under the name Dawn O'Neill.

If you want to learn more about her, try following her on social media:
Instagram: kimberly_oneill
Twitter: @koneillwriter
Facebook: @oneillk
YouTube: Kimberly O'Neill - Writer